THE TATTOOED POTATO AND OTHER CLUES

WANTED: Assistant to well-known portrait painter.

THE SCENE: New York City and a sky-lighted artist's studio in an old Greenwich Village house—charming, except for the two criminals on the first floor and a monster in the basement.

THE JOB: Art apprentice, keeper of disguises, spy, detective, eyewitness to murder.

THE CHARACTERS: Garson (alias Inspector Noserag), fashionable portrait painter and self-acclaimed "greatest sleuth in the universe." Dickory Dock (alias Sergeant Kod), first-year art student. And Chief Detective Quinn, Manny Mallomar, Shrimps Marinara, and many others.

INCLUDING: The Case of the Horrible Hairdresser, The Case of the Face on the Five Dollar Bill, The Case of the Full-Sized Midget, and The Case of the Disguised Disguise.

"Daffy detection with a sharp eye to penetrating disguises."
—*School Library Journal*

Also by Ellen Raskin

Figgs & Phantoms
The Mysterious Disappearance of Leon (I mean Noel)

ELLEN RASKIN

The Tattooed Potato
and other clues

Puffin Books

PUFFIN BOOKS
Published by the Penguin Group
Viking Penguin Inc., 40 West 23rd Street, New York, New York 10010, U.S.A.
Penguin Books Ltd, 27 Wrights Lane, London W8 5TZ, England
Penguin Books Australia Ltd, Ringwood, Victoria, Australia
Penguin Books Canada Ltd, 2801 John Street, Markham, Ontario, Canada L3R 1B4
Penguin Books (N.Z.) Ltd, 182–190 Wairau Road, Auckland 10, New Zealand

Penguin Books Ltd, Registered Offices: Harmondsworth, Middlesex, England

First published in the United States of America by E.P. Dutton, a division of NAL Penguin Inc., 1975
Published in Puffin Books 1989
10 9 8 7 6 5 4 3 2 1

LIBRARY OF CONGRESS CATALOGING IN PUBLICATION DATA
Raskin, Ellen.
    The tattooed potato and other clues / by Ellen Raskin   p.   cm.
Summary: Answering an advertisement for an artist's assistant involves
seventeen-year-old Dickory Dock in several mysteries and their ultimate solutions.
ISBN 0–14–032980–3
[1. Mystery and detective stories.]   I. Title.
PZ7.R1817Tat 1989   —[Fic]—dc19

Printed in the United States of America by R.R. Donnelley & Sons Company, Harrisonburg, VA
Set in Baskerville

CONTENTS

?

The Mystery in
Number 12 Cobble Lane

1

A lonely figure stood in Cobble Lane, studying the red-brick house numbered 12. Nervously she clicked a broken fingernail.

No signs of life could be seen behind the muntined (was that the right word?) windows framed by quaint, blue-green shutters. No people, no cars troubled this shy Greenwich Village street.

Only Dickory.

Dickory had never been in Cobble Lane before, although she had lived all of her seventeen years just one mile away—one mile away in a decaying tenement that rumbled with passing trucks and shuddered above the subway's roar. Here, hidden by the lane's narrow bend, these small, historic houses stood huddled in silence, untouched by the frantic city that had grown up around them.

Fumbling through her shoulder bag, the trespasser found the notice she had removed from the school bulletin board that morning.

WANTED

Art student to assist well-known
portrait painter.
3–6 Mon–Fri, all day Sat.   Good pay.
Must be native New Yorker,
neat, well-organized.
QUIET! OBSERVANT!
Apply: Garson.   12 Cobble Lane.

Dickory wanted that job. But what if Garson asked to see her portfolio? It was one thing to get accepted into art school with street scenes done with Magic Markers, but. . . . Dickory bit off the ragged edge of her fingernail. How would she introduce herself if Garson, himself, answered the door? She would say nothing, just hand him the notice. She would be quiet.

Quiet and observant.

Observant Dickory counted the windows: ten in all, three on the second floor, two on the first floor, two in the—someone was watching her from a basement window. No, no one was there. It seemed as if the house itself was watching her as she clutched the cast-iron newel, climbed the one-two-three steps of the brownstone stoop, rang the bell, and waited before the eight-paneled door, painted the same blue-green as the shutters.

At last a bolt lock turned. A man in blue jeans opened the door and took the notice from her outstretched hand.

"Come in. I'm Garson."

Silent Dickory stepped into the old house to become paint-sorter, brush-cleaner, treasure-keeper, spy, detective, and once again companion to murder.

Double murder.

Dickory followed the artist down the dimly lit hall, through a door at the foot of steep and straight stairs. Unlike the narrow entranceway, the double-storied, oak-paneled room that lay before her was massive. Standing at a carved balustrade, she gaped at the tall, arched windows, the huge, stone fireplace, the antique furniture and Oriental rugs.

"Not that way," Garson said as she started down the short, curved steps to the magnificent room. "Oh, well, I guess you should have a tour, in case of fire. Or some other emergency." His tour consisted of a few bored waves of his hand. "Over there, at the far end of the living room, is the garden door. The kitchen is down here under this balcony. Through the kitchen is the furnace room, storeroom, and guest room. A door under the front stoop opens to the street."

Dickory tried to remember: kitchen under balcony, furnace room, storeroom, guest room, outside door.

"Two men will be taking over these rooms tomorrow; I'm moving to the top two floors. Come, there's packing to do." Garson turned and led her into the front bedroom, whose windows looked upon Cobble Lane.

Dickory wondered why Garson had to move upstairs; but she asked nothing.

"Good, you are quiet," he said. "Quiet people don't ask questions."

Dickory had passed her first test.

Trying to be "neat and well-organized," Dickory began packing the contents of the closets and drawers into large cartons. A baggy clown suit. A bullfighter's beaded jacket. A sequined ball gown, very daring.

"Are you a native New Yorker?" Garson asked. He was leaning against the wall, hands halfway into the pockets of his custom-fitted jeans.

"Yes." Dickory placed a ballerina's tutu into a carton.

Garson nodded. "Then you won't be afraid of opening the front door to strangers. That would be one of your duties, answering the door. And the telephone. And cleaning paintbrushes and palettes, etcetera."

Silently, Dickory folded a black opera cape on top of a sailor's middy. What did he mean by "etcetera"? And what kind of strangers came to his front door? She reached to the top shelf of the closet for wigs and toupees of all colors and textures, hats and caps of all types and times.

Garson straightened and turned to leave. "By the way, what's your name?"

"Dickory," she replied, staring into a drawer stuffed with monocles and medals, eye patches and false teeth.

"Is that your first name or last?"

Dickory sighed. That was not a fair question from a man who called himself Garson, just Garson. "My last name is Dock," she replied combatively, waiting for the usual guffaw.

Garson didn't even smile.

Closets and drawers emptied, four large cartons packed, Dickory stood at the foot of the steep hall stairs. Garson had told her to "Give a yell" when she was done, but what should she yell? What do you call someone who has only one name? "Garson" seemed too familiar; "Hey, mister" too crass; "Yoo-hoo" too cute. "Boss"? She didn't even have the job, yet.

Dickory returned to the bedroom and dragged, shoved, bumped a heavy carton along the floor, over the sill, and through the door. She paused to arch her aching back, waiting for Garson to appear. Surely he must have heard the noise she had made.

Suddenly Dickory became aware of footsteps in the apartment she had just left. Thudding feet clumped up the curved staircase from the living room, coming closer, closer toward the darkening door.

Cringing against the hallway wall, Dickory stared up at a huge, disfigured monster of a man. A jagged scar cut across his smashed face, twisting his mouth into a horrible grin, blinding one eye white and unblinking.

Dickory screamed. The giant lumbered toward her, arms outstretched, fingers jerking wildly. She screamed again.

"I didn't expect you to take me so literally when I said 'Give a yell,' " Garson said flatly from the top of the stairs. "Oh, I see Isaac is helping out."

The awful Isaac bent down, flipped the carton onto a massive shoulder, and carried it up to the studio floor. Trembling, Dickory sank down on the bottom step.

"Sorry, I should have told you about Isaac Bicker-staffe," Garson said, nonchalantly tripping down the stairs. "He lives in the guest room under the front stoop. Isaac is quite harmless and . . . are you all right?"

"I'm fine, just fine," Dickory replied, pulling herself up by the banister. "After all, I am a native New Yorker."

"Exactly."

Dickory followed the portrait painter into the bare bedroom. His tailored jeans were now smeared with paint. He had changed his expensive loafers for dirty sneakers, his starched shirt for a metallic-blue turtleneck jersey. Cold blue, like his eyes.

Garson surveyed the empty room and nodded his approval. "What time is it?"

Dickory looked at the cheaply made, poorly designed

wristwatch her brother had given her as a high school graduation present. "It's a quarter to six, more or less."

Garson frowned. "I have an important dinner party to go to, so the observancy test will have to wait until tomorrow. Ever hear of the Panzpresser Collection?"

"Yes." Dickory had never heard of the Panzpresser Collection, but she had something else on her mind. The room was too clean.

"Best private collection of Post-Impressionist paintings in this country. Not that I much care for that school. As far as I'm concerned, art stopped with Fragonard."

Isaac had returned. Garson pointed to the three remaining cartons, then continued. "Anyhow, Julius Panzpresser is the collector, but his wife is the one with taste. She wants me to paint her portrait."

Dickory studied the planked floor. Either Garson was joking, which seemed unlikely, or he was a pompous fool, a phony. She kept her head down while Isaac stacked the cartons and carried them out of the room. She could not bear to look at the disfigured creature, and she certainly did not want to be formally introduced.

"Let's call it a day," Garson said.

Dickory protested feebly. "I thought I would unpack while you dress for your dinner party. The costumes will get wrinkled if. . . ."

"But I *have* changed," Garson replied. "The Panzpressers invited an artist, and they are going to get an artist."

He was a phony, Dickory decided, as she followed him out the front door.

A taxi was waiting at the curb. "Where do you live?" Garson asked, doubling his long legs into the back seat.

"First Avenue and Fourteenth Street," Dickory replied, hoping for a ride home. "With my brother and his wife."

"Have a pleasant walk." He slammed the door.

Shivering in the early evening chill, Dickory watched the cab drive off, then started on the mile-walk home. She had to walk. She had accidentally packed her purse and jacket in one of the costume cartons.

2

"Who's Dick Ory?" Professor D'Arches pointed to one of the color compositions propped before the design class.

"The name is Dickory," She had intentionally signed her name to look like two.

"Do you know what you've done here, Dickory?"

"Not really," she admitted. Using four different Magic Markers, she had composed a square of joined triangles, but it had been difficult working in yellows by candlelight amidst the bickering and squabbling. Her brother and sister-in-law had argued most of the night about who was supposed to have paid the electric bill, and they had argued into the morning and through a breakfast of boiled coffee and untoasted bread over which one of them had spent the money saved to pay the bill. Now, in daylight, Dickory's color arrangement looked quite different. The yellow triangles were almost indistinguishable from one another.

"A monochromatic design could have included tones and shades, you know," the professor said. "What do you call this masterpiece, 'Yellow on Yellow'?"

Dickory didn't respond. No one responded. D'Arches shook his head in despair. "That was a clever pun, but obviously none of you self-styled artists has ever heard of Malevich's 'White on White,' let alone Futurism or Suprematism." He sighed. "All right, which genius wants to give his opinion of Dickory's work?"

A freckled, gangling youth rose and raised his hand. "I think it is very subtle, sir."

The class giggled at his polite high school manner.

"And which of these disasters is yours?" D'Arches asked.

"The purple one, sir."

"Well, well, it seems we have a Fauve in our midst. Or is it Naïf?"

"Pardon, sir?"

The professor read the signature on the clumsy arrangement in purple, violet, and lavender. "Sit down, George the Third."

The blushing young man resumed his seat and smiled at Dickory.

"If this class spent more time on design, and less time on their signatures, I wouldn't be ruining my digestion on such garbage." D'Arches pointed to a green composition thick with pigments squeezed from the tube. "Where's the plagarist who signs himself 'Vincent'?"

A bearded student defiantly explained that Vincent was his middle name.

"It is also the signature of Vincent Van Gogh," the professor replied angrily. "Isn't anyone here original enough to sign his own name? Where's the joker who thinks he's Whistler?"

"That signature is not a butterfly," a chubby young man argued. "It's a silverfish. Harold Silverfish is the name."

"Get out of here, all of you, this minute. Out!"

Avoiding George III, who wanted to talk to her, Dickory hurried into the library. Professor D'Arches' short temper had given her an extra half hour before she was due in Cobble Lane, time enough to find out about the Panzpresser Collection and Fragonard. And Garson.

Panzpresser, Julius. 1905–   . Art collector and retired clothing manufacturer. Wife's name: Cookie. Homes in Manhattan and Palm Beach. Art collection, worth $12 million, includes paintings by Degas, Gauguin, Toulouse-Lautrec, Van Gogh, Matisse, Picasso, Sonneborg.

The artists' names were familiar to her, except the last. She had never heard of Sonneborg, but she had never heard of Fragonard, either.

Fragonard, Jean Honoré. 1732–1806. French painter.

Dickory flipped through the reproductions of Fragonard paintings. The colors were too sweet for her taste, the subject matter too shallow; but she had to admire his drawing skill.

Next, Garson. Dickory had searched through four biographical dictionaries of American artists before she found one short entry.

> Garson. 1935– . American portrait painter. Born: Pigslop, Iowa. Father's name: Gar. Occupation: macaroni designer. Mother's maiden name: Aurora Borealis. Studied in Paris at L'Ecole de Louvre. Among the celebrities held in posterity under his facile brush are: Juanita Chiquita Dobson, banana heiress. . . .

Dickory slammed the book shut. Just in case there was some truth among those outrageous lies, she looked up two other names. There was no Pigslop in Iowa; there was no L'Ecole de Louvre. She had discovered only one thing about her possible employer: Garson wanted no one to know anything about Garson.

Steeling herself against the possibility of Isaac answering the door, Dickory rang the bell at Number 12 Cobble Lane. But neither Isaac nor Garson appeared. A fat man filled the doorway, a very fat man with bulging eyes and greasy skin that took on a purplish cast next to his white suit. His shirt, his tie, even his shoes were white. "White on White," Dickory thought.

"Come on up," Garson called from the landing.

Still blocking the entrance, the fat man scowled. "You the kid that's supposed to answer the door? Next time you're late, I'm kicking you out on your can."

Ignoring his greeting, Dickory squeezed past and slowly, haughtily climbed the stairs. The fat man muttered some indistinct curses and slammed the door to the downstairs apartment. His apartment, now.

"I see you've met Manny Mallomar," Garson said, leading her into his studio.

Her distaste for the repulsive new tenant was immediately washed away in a flood of light. Head raised to the enormous skylight that slanted two stories above her, Dickory turned in a circle between two large oak easels and blinked into the bright daylight. It was brighter than daylight, free of the glare and the shadows of the sun.

"Haven't you ever seen a skylight before?" Garson asked.

"Not like this. There's a tiny skylight in our bathroom that leaks when it rains, but the landlord won't fix it. 'Why fix it?' he says. 'What's a little water, more or less, in a bathroom?'" Dickory stopped, remembering that she was supposed to be quiet.

Garson was neither disapproving nor sympathetic. "That makes sense," he said, and beckoned her to the open staircase that hugged one of the studio walls.

Reminding herself to be observant, Dickory glanced about the spacious floor. There were no partitions dividing the front part of the house, now a library, from the glass-roofed studio, only a kitchen area against the opposite wall.

"Come," Garson urged. "The cartons are up here."

At the top of the stairs Dickory once again stood on a balcony. This one was much higher and looked into the skylight and down upon the easels. She thought she saw a man in colorful clothes sitting in a chair, but Garson quickly led her away from the railing and down a narrow hall.

"That's my bedroom, the bathroom is over there, and this is the spare room. I'll store the costumes in here for the while."

The four unopened cartons were piled in the center of the small room. Garson pointed to the bare closets and empty chest of drawers. Dickory noticed a slight but un-mistakable tremor in his right hand.

"I'm sure you've learned to be better organized after your walk home." He had known about her missing purse and jacket all along. Avoiding his stare, Dickory opened the top box and removed a huntsman's coat. Garson moved toward the door. "I'm going down to work. I've got to finish my lawyer's portrait so I can begin painting Cookie Panzpresser. I'll be back later to find out how observant you are."

Trying to memorize the inventory as she unpacked, Dickory separated the men's costumes from the women's and arranged them in a vague historical sequence. In the middle of the third carton, between a lumberjack shirt and a red feather boa, she found her jacket and shoul-der bag.

"How's it going?"

Dickory jumped. "Fine," she replied, stooping to pick up the ruffled parasol that had fallen to the floor. "I'm nearly finished."

Garson inspected the closets and drawers, then leaned against the wall. Ice cubes clinked against the glass in his hand. "Now let's see how observant you are. I'll give you three questions, and if you answer them correctly, the job is yours. No, don't turn around, just keep doing what you're doing."

She was kneeling on the closet floor, lining up high-buttoned shoes, beaded slippers, and fur-trimmed boots.

"Do you know the difference between a primitive painter and a creative artist?" Garson asked.

Surprised, Dickory spun around. She had expected to be questioned about the costumes or the house or the Panzpresser Collection or Fragonard.

"Sorry, I didn't mean that to be a question; I'm just

explaining the rules of the game." Dickory returned to the shoes. "The difference is this," Garson explained, "the primitive painter meticulously draws in every brick on a building because he knows the bricks are there. But the creative artist can suggest bricks with a few strokes of his brush. The creative artist is concerned, not with facades, but with the inner structure, with the truth of what he sees."

Dickory polished the toe of a cowboy boot with the sleeve of her sweatshirt. She had meticulously drawn every brick in her Magic Marker street scenes.

"Seeing the structure behind the facade, seeing the truth behind the disguise, that's what I mean by being observant," Garson said. "Remember that in answering my questions. Understand?"

"Yes." That sounded simple enough.

"All right, then. In one word, only one word, describe Isaac Bickerstaffe."

"Who?" Dickory stalled for time.

"Isaac, the man who lives under the front stoop."

"Oh." Dickory sat back on her heels and closed her eyes. She shuddered at the remembered features of the misshapen giant.

"Take your time," Garson said between sips of his drink. "But remember—one word, the most important word."

Isaac Bickerstaffe seemed too big to squeeze into one word. "Scarface" didn't indicate his size, neither did "one-eyed." On the other hand, "huge" or "giant" didn't indicate his scars. Or his scariness. "Monster," that was it.

"Monster," Dickory said.

Garson shook his head. "You disappoint me. Poor, gentle Isaac a monster? That is not only inaccurate, it's uncharitable. The word for Isaac is 'deaf-mute.' "

Now Dickory remembered the flying fingers, the vacant stare. Shamed by her stupidity, she stood up as her hopes for the job crashed down around her. She decided to fight for another chance. "Deaf mute is two words," she challenged.

"One word," Garson replied. "Deaf-hyphen-mute."

"But Isaac Bickerstaffe is more than just a deaf-hyphen-mute." This was her last try.

Garson stared into his empty glass. "Yes, Isaac is also brain-damaged." There was compassion in his voice, but when he looked up his face wore the same blank mask. "Ready for the next question?" He pointed a shaky finger at the shoes.

Again kneeling on the closet floor, Dickory paired a Greek sandal with an Indian moccasin.

"In one word, and only one word, describe the new tenant, Manny Mallomar."

She had to do better this time, but "gross" fought with "greasy," "foul-mouthed" with "white-suited." Only one word described both the man and his character.

"Ugly," she said.

"I, myself, would have said 'fat,' " Garson replied. "Mallomar could never hide his obesity, no matter what his disguise. But I'll accept 'ugly'; only the brush of a portrait painter could disguise that."

Why was he always talking about disguises?

"Now, take Manny Mallomar again, and step by step describe what cannot be disguised. Forget about 'ugly' this time."

"Fat," she began. That word had already been approved. "Bulging eyes."

"He could hide his pop-eyes behind dark glasses," Garson said.

"About five-feet eight-inches tall."

"Mallomar wears stacked-heel shoes and is only five-five."

"White stacked-heel shoes," Dickory continued, "white shirt, white suit, white tie."

"He could change his clothes."

"Greasy skin, dark-complected."

"The word is complexioned, not complected. And he could change his skin color with makeup."

Defeated at every turn, Dickory blurted: "Manny Mallomar looks like the ghost of a greasy hamburger."

"Not bad, Dickory. Imaginative, even creative; but you still have a lot to learn about being observant. Think of it this way: if Manny Mallomar walked through that door in bare feet, wearing a dark blue suit, sunglasses, and makeup, how would you recognize him?"

"Fat."

"Are you sure he's fat? He could be padded."

Dickory was tiring of the game. "I would recognize Manny Mallomar by the thick roll of fat at the back of his neck, by his fat fingers, and by his fat thighs that make him stand with his feet wide apart."

"You are an apt pupil." With that, Garson left the room. He told her to come down to the studio for the third question when she had finished unpacking the costumes.

Costumes? Why would a painter of distinguished men and wealthy women keep such a gaudy wardrobe, Dickory wondered. Were they really costumes, or were they disguises?

Arranging painted fans and junk jewelry in the last drawer, Dickory thought about the third question. She knew what it would be, and she knew that she was being given time to think about it.

What was the one word that described Garson?

Dickory pictured his regular, expressionless features: blue eyes; blond hair, longish and styled; thin lips that never smiled; fair skin, unwrinkled, slightly blotched. Voice: flat, almost bored, except when he spoke of art or Isaac. Size: tall, but not unusually so; lean. Clothes: starched shirt tapered to cling to his slim waist; sleeves rolled high on taut, tanned arms; tailored blue jeans, tight-fitting. He probably worked out in a gym to keep in such fine trim.

"Trim," that was a good word. At least it was better than "phony."

"Come on down," Garson called. He had a fresh drink in one hand, a paintbrush in the other.

"Dissipated," Dickory thought, descending the open staircase. Then she remembered what he had said about the Mallomar descriptions. There was only one thing about Garson that could not be disguised: the tremor in his right hand.

Once again Dickory stood under the immense skylight. Garson was painting at one easel, the other easel was covered with a red velvet drape. What she had thought was a man sitting in the chair was not a man at all, but a life-sized artist's manikin dressed in jockey silks.

Dickory watched Garson lay a rosy glaze on the cheek of the distinguished, gray-suited lawyer. His brush was sure and steady; his hand no longer shook. Rejecting the word "hand-tremor," she was now confronted with another hyphenated word: "third-rate." Garson was a third-rate painter. Although competent, the portrait he was painting said nothing about the lawyer, nothing about the artist. It was a slick and shallow illustration. Perhaps "slick" was more charitable than "third-rate," or should she return to "trim"?

"Ready for the last question?" Garson stepped back to squint at his canvas. "Now, in one word and only one word, describe. . . ."

A bell rang. "Excuse me," Dickory said. She hastened out of the studio and down the hall stairs, thankful that one of her duties was to open the front door to strangers.

A little man in black scampered through the front door and into Mallomar's apartment. His overcoat, over-long and overlarge, surrounded him like a carapace. Beady eyes darted suspiciously between his wide-brimmed hat and upturned collar. He seemed to move sideways, like a crab. No, "crab" sounded too threatening for that inconspicuous little shrimp.

"Who was at the door?" Garson asked.

"Shrimp," Dickory replied.

Garson nodded, intent on his canvas. "That's the other new tenant." Suddenly he spun around. "Did he tell you his name?"

"No, not unless his name is Out-of-My-Way-Punk."

Garson threw back his head and crowed a cheer that sounded like "yee-ick-hooo," then raced around his studio looking for something called a mahlstick. Thinking he had lost his senses, Dickory pretended to search.

"Ah, here it is." He walked toward her, holding the long aluminum rod with a balled end that easel painters use as a handrest when brushing in fine details. Raising the mahlstick high into the air, he brought it down with a light tap on Dickory's shoulder. "Dickory Dock," he announced solemnly, "I dub you Apprentice to Garson."

Dickory looked puzzled.

"You're hired, Dickory. The name of the little man you so accurately described is Shrimps Marinara."

3

Apprenticed and awarded the keys to the house, Dickory was set to the task of cleaning the taboret that stood next to the velvet-draped easel.

"Roy G. Biv," Garson said when he opened the taboret drawers to show her where the pigments were stored. That's all he said: Roy G. Biv. He said nothing more about the artist who painted at that easel nor why the canvas was covered, and Dickory did not ask. That Roy G. Biv was an artist with messy working habits was obvious from the scruffy brushes stiff with paint and the haphazardly squeezed tubes that lay in disarray, uncapped and oozing, on the dirty cabinet top.

Dickory found the matching cap for a tube of cadmium orange and screwed it on tightly, then Naples yellow, while Garson applied glaze upon glaze to the lawyer's handsome face. Unlike Roy G. Biv, Garson was extremely neat; his working area, clean and well-organized.

For the next several days Garson neither spoke nor acknowledged Dickory's presence as he painted the uninspired portrait. Dickory capped and recapped the same tubes of cadmium orange and Naples yellow. Every evening she left the second taboret clean, only to return the following afternoon to a sticky, smeary mess.

No stranger came to the door; the telephone did not ring. Except for Manny Mallomar swearing at Isaac Bickerstaffe, who was helping him move some heavy filing cabinets into the downstairs apartment, the afternoons were silent. Oppressively silent. At one point Dickory almost started a conversation with the manikin seated in the chair before her, the larger-than-life jockey in orange and yellow silks.

Cadmium orange. Naples yellow. Roy G. Biv was painting the jockey, but she had yet to see either the artist or his canvas that was hidden under the velvet drape.

Dickory did meet a familiar figure leaving the studio when she arrived one day—a balding, sour-faced man with blubbery lips. Only after some effort did she recognize him as the lawyer in Garson's painting, who had come for his last sitting. His ugliness had been well-disguised by the artist's brush.

"What time is it, Dickory?"

Surprised to hear Garson speak, Dickory looked at her bare wrist. "I don't know. I pawned my watch to help pay the electric bill."

"Just as well," he said, adding a glaze of shadow to firm the lawyer's lips. "It was an ugly watch anyhow."

Garson did not speak again until the middle of Friday afternoon. "Almost finished," he announced, stepping back from his canvas. "Come take a look."

Dickory glanced at the lawyer's glowing face. "Almost finished," she agreed, and returned to Roy G. Biv's messy taboret. It was the kindest opinion she could give of the third-rate, no, fourth-rate painting. Head down, she could hear Garson swishing his brush in solvent; she could feel his critical stare.

"You're a strange one, Dickory," he said evenly. "Unreachable—wait, that's not the right word."

Dickory waited. What was the right word for her? She wished she had been able to wash her hair that morning, but the kitchen sink was full of dishes and her sister-in-law's uniform was soaking in the tub. Anyhow, "dirty hair" was two words. So was "ragged fingernails," "roundish face," "flattish nose." Nervously she screwed a yellow cap on an orange paint tube.

"I have it; I have the word for you, Dickory," Garson said at last. "The word for you is 'haunted.' "

Haunted? Dickory looked into the tall oval mirror that stood on bracketed feet in a corner of the studio. A haunted face framed by dirty hair looked back at her.

"Haunted," Garson repeated. "Haunted by self-doubt. Haunted by some tragedy. A haunted angel from another world. You are a Piero della Francesca angel."

That was someone else she had to find out about, Piero della Francesca, along with Roy G. Biv.

With a tiny brush and a steady hand, Garson painted a carnation in the lawyer's lapel. He did not use his mahlstick. Perhaps he kept the mahlstick only for tapping apprentices, Dickory thought.

"Of course, a little self-doubt is a good thing if you want to become an artist, a good artist," Garson said.

"Makes you work harder. Work and study, experimentation, devotion—that's what you need to develop a style of your own. You can learn techniques, but no one can teach you style."

Dickory had no intention of learning Garson's slick style, but she was learning about paints by watching him and cleaning up after Roy G. Biv. She seemed to be the only one in her class without a working knowledge of art materials.

"What I can teach you is how to observe," Garson continued. "How to see through frills and facades; how to see through disguises. How to see with an artist's eye. And the simplest way to teach that is to play our little game."

"Describing?" Dickory asked, hoping it was not her turn to give the one word for Garson.

"That's right, describing. From now on I want a description of every person who visits Manny Mallomar. You can use more than one word, if necessary, but always remember to look beyond the disguise. And get their names, too, if you can. Understand?"

"Yes." To Dickory it seemed more like spying than a lesson or a game. But spying on whom? And for what purpose?

The doorbell rang only once that day. Dickory noticed Mallomar peering suspiciously through his half-opened door when she let his nervous visitor into the house.

"Turkey-necked Mr. Smith," she reported to Garson.

"Very good," he remarked sadly.

Greenwich Village sleeps until noon on weekends. Alone, Dickory walked through silent streets, past barricaded shops. But someone else was already in Cobble

Lane when she turned into its narrow bend. A derelict, unshaven chin on his chest, sat sprawled on the stoop of the house opposite Number 12.

No longer a trespasser, Dickory resented the intrusions of the rude and ugly tenants, and now a filthy drunk. Unlocking the front door, she turned to give him a disapproving look, but the drunk, too, was asleep.

Although bleary-eyed, Garson was awake, slouched in a wing chair in the library. He waved his coffee cup at her to join him.

"There's a dirty drunk outside," she complained.

"Haven't you ever seen a derelict before?"

"Sure, there's always one or two asleep in our foyer, but that's different."

Garson shrugged. "Forget it, he's not hurting anyone. Sit down, I have something for you." He pushed an oblong box across the tabletop.

It was a wristwatch, tastefully designed, its clean and open face in ideal proportion to its wide black strap. Dickory buckled it to her wrist. "Thank you."

"Don't you like it?"

"Yes, it's very nice."

"Haunted Dickory Dock," Garson said, studying her intently. "Now, let's see. You have known another watch, a more beautiful watch, in that other world of yours."

Amazed at Garson's perception, Dickory had to admit he was right. "It was an antique. In an enameled case with roses painted on it. And it played a tune."

Garson seemed interested. "Was it yours?"

Dickory shook her head. "It was going to be my high school graduation present. A few years back a student came into my parents' shop, Dock's Hock Shop. He wanted to pawn some art books, and that watch. My father said he didn't buy books, and my mother said the watch was an antique—beautiful, but with no real value. I was in the store helping out that day, and I made a big fuss about wanting that watch more than anything in the world. So, my dad bought it and promised to give it to me if I finished high school. He had to take the art books, too. That's when I decided to become an artist, after studying the books and. . . ." Dickory bit her lip. She was talking too much, and sharing her secrets.

"What happened to the watch?" Garson asked.

"Robbery."

"And your parents?"

"Murdered."

Garson stood up and walked to the door of his studio. He closed it, something he had never done before in her presence. "Do you remember the tune the watch played?"

Dickory sipped her coffee to compose herself and wet her dry mouth, then she whistled the tune.

"I know that song." Leaning against the closed door, hands behind him on the knob, Garson softly sang the words:

" 'Oranges and lemons,'
     say the bells of St. Clements;
'You owe me five farthings,'
     say the bells of St. Martins;
'When will you pay me?'
     say the bells of Old Bailey;
'When I grow rich,'
     say the bells of Shoreditch;
'When will that be?'
     say the bells of Stepney;
'I do not know,'
     says the great bell of Bow.
Here comes a candle to light you to bed,
And here comes a chopper to chop off your head!"

Another bell rang, the doorbell. The artist opened the door for Dickory, who slowly descended the hall stairs.

A hearty, middle-aged man asked to see Garson. Ruddy skin (no makeup), thinning gray hair (his own), no more than five-feet ten-inches tall, solid (no padding), neatly dressed in a brown suit, brown polka-dot tie. Tomorrow he might wear a blue suit and blue tie, but they would still be flecked with cigar ashes; for, protruding from his mouth as if it were part of his face, was a half-smoked, well-chewed cigar.

Dickory asked his name.

"Joseph P. Quinn," he said, shifting his cigar. "Chief of Detectives, New York City Police."

The Case of the
Horrible Hairdresser

1

"I need the artist whose eyes can see through disguise," Chief of Detectives Joseph P. Quinn said jovially. "I've given some thought to what you said at the Panzpressers' party, and I'm here to test your theory. It's my last resort."

"Must have had too much champagne; I don't remember what I said." Garson seemed annoyed with himself for having confided in the police.

"You said that in the case of a clever criminal descriptions are useless, unless the eyewitness is questioned by an artist," Quinn explained. "You said that a clever criminal can make people see only what he wants them to see."

Garson frowned.

"You also said that if I brought the witnesses to you, you could paint a portrait from their descriptions that would be much closer to the truth than any portrait a police artist could make."

Garson's hand shook.

The chief looked at Dickory. "Could I have some of that coffee, Miss, um. . . ."

Garson formally introduced them. "Chief Joseph P. Quinn, this is my apprentice, Dickory Dock."

Joseph P. Quinn laughed heartily. "Hickory Dickory Dock, now how does that go?

> "Hickory Dickory Dock,
>   The mouse ran up the clock,
>   The clock struck one,
>   The mouse fell down. . . .

"No, that's not right; 'down' doesn't rhyme with 'one.' Let me see—one–done–fun–gun. . . ."

"You were saying something about testing my theory, Chief," Garson said quickly, afraid that Dickory was about to pour the coffee on Quinn's lap.

"What? Oh yes, your theory. I've got a tough case on my hands, Garson; and I thought maybe you could help me out by questioning the three eyewitnesses." Chief Quinn gulped down his coffee, rose and wandered about the studio to allow Garson time to make his decision. He stopped at the finished portrait and studied the lawyer's face with interest. "Say, you *are* an artist, Garson. This picture is good, really good. It looks realistic, not like those smears that pass for art these days. I like it."

The chief sounded sincere, but why shouldn't he be, Dickory thought. Anyone who recited nursery rhymes was bound to like Garson's slick and superficial style.

Quinn joined Dickory at the window overlooking Cobble Lane. "I've got it:

"Hickory Dickory Dock,
The mouse ran up the clock,
The clock struck one,
And down he run,
Just like Hickory Dickory Dock.

"How's that? Get it—down he run, just like you run down to answer the door."

Dickory's eyes remained on the street below. The derelict was still sprawled on the stoop, flagrantly ignoring the policeman-chauffeur behind the wheel of the chief's car. "Are you going to arrest that drunk, Chief Quinn?"

Quinn shifted his cigar. "He doesn't seem to be bothering anybody, does he? You know, Hickory, if we arrested derelicts there'd be no room left in our jails for the real criminals." Dickory brushed ashes from her shoulder as the chief turned to leave. "Well, Garson, are you going to help me out with the witnesses?"

Garson nodded somewhat reluctantly. "Bring them here at three this afternoon."

"Good. Three o'clock, then. And thanks." Quinn stopped at the studio door. "By the way, I call this one The Case of the Horrible Hairdresser."

Garson remained in his chair silently thinking, drinking his second pot of coffee. Dickory cleaned up after Roy G. Biv. Three times the doorbell rang; three people, all wearing dark glasses, had come to see Manny Mallomar: wobble-hipped Mrs. Jones, stilt-legged Mrs. Smith, and finger-cracking Mr. Smith.

"Don't bother, it's waterproof," Garson said as she was about to remove her new watch to wash the turpentine-cleaned brushes in the kitchen sink. "Besides, it's almost lunchtime. Run over to the deli and bring back some sandwiches; charge it to my account."

Wondering about horrible hairdressers and why Mallomar's guests were named either Smith or Jones, Dickory sauntered to the delicatessen around the corner. "Corned beef on rye with lots of mustard, and cole slaw, and extra pickle slices," she ordered for herself. She paused. What kind of sandwich would someone like Gar son want? Something bland and humorless. "Turkey on thin-sliced white bread, no mayonnaise."

Back on Cobble Lane she ignored the derelict's plea for spare change and hurried into the house to be greeted by another repugnant character in the dimly lit hall. Manny Mallomar grabbed Dickory by her jacket collar. "What was that cop doing upstairs?"

"Ask him yourself; he'll be back any minute." Dickory pushed against the fat man, squirming out of his grasp, and climbed the stairs in time to his muttered profanities. Mallomar had squashed her sandwiches, but he had also stained his white suit with pickle juice.

Garson was still deep in thought when Dickory slapped the soggy lunch bag on the kitchen counter. "All right!" he exclaimed, aloud but to himself. He clapped his hands on the arms of his chair and stood up. He had made a decision. "Let's fix up this place and get ready for the eyewitnesses. Detectives must be well-organized for detecting and deducting." With a hammer he banged against the radiator under the front window, setting up ear-shattering and floor-shaking reverberations. Then he listened. Stunned, Dickory removed her hands from her ears and listened, too.

Mallomar shouted up some ugliness, then heavy thuds climbed the stairs.

"Isaac can feel the vibrations in his basement room," he explained to his cringing apprentice as the one-eyed mute lumbered into the studio. Garson wrote the lawyer's name in large block letters on a sheet of paper, handed it to Isaac, and pointed to the portrait. Isaac left with the large canvas tucked under one arm.

"Can he read?" Dickory asked hoarsely, still trembling.

"A bit. He engraves my name and the sitter's name on a gold plaque after he finishes the frame."

"He makes your frames?"

Garson nodded. When he spoke again, his voice was touched with sadness. "No one knows anything about that poor lost soul—who he was or what he did before some terrible accident tore apart his face and mangled his brain. Isaac, himself, remembers nothing, but his fingers have not forgotten their craft."

"Then how do you know his name is Isaac Bickerstaffe?" Dickory persisted.

"Questions, questions," Garson replied sharply. "No more questions, please remember that."

Dickory shrugged.

Garson sighed. "Haunted Dickory. I'll tell you what— I'll answer your question if you promise it will be your last."

Too proud to promise anything, Dickory stared at him blankly. Garson turned and busied himself in the studio, arranging three straight-backed chairs between the empty easel and the draped easel. Then he started up the open stairway but stopped in midflight, having decided to answer her question. "I named him myself," he said, leaning over the banister. "I named him Isaac Bickerstaffe after an obscure nineteenth-century poet, who wrote:

"I care for nobody, no, not I,
 If nobody cares for me.

"I thought that sentiment suited the expression on his battered face. Now, no more questions. Get out a pen and a notebook; I'll be right down."

A different Garson came down the stairs. Although still unsmiling, this one seemed more sprightly, almost playful. He was carrying a paint-smeared smock, an artist's beret, and two other hats.

"Hats?" asked Dickory, notebook in hand. Realizing it was a question, she changed her tone. "Hats," she said affirmatively.

"Right you are, Sergeant Kod. These are hats."

"And I am Sergeant Kod," Dickory guessed.

"Right again." Garson placed a bobby's helmet on her head, a deerstalker hat on his.

"And you are Sherlock Holmes."

"Wrong," he replied. "I am Inspector Noserag."

"Noserag?!" That was funnier than Dickory Dock.

"Simple, actch-ly," Garson said in near-British accents. "Noserag is Garson spelled backward, almost. And Kod is Dock spelled backward, almost."

"And we are almost detectives," said Dickory.

"We ARE detectives, Sergeant Kod. I am the greatest sleuth in the universe, and you are my trusted assistant."

Pacing the floor, the greatest sleuth in the universe dictated a list of art supplies to his trusted assistant, who wrote out an accurate list in spite of the difficulties she had understanding Noserag's accent, which alternated between British and Humphrey Bogart: a new easel, taboret, life-sized manikin, brushes, paints.

"Acrylics," he said, now British. "Indeed, I surmise acrylic paints would be preferable, more synonymous with the precision of modern detection." The inspector inspected Dickory's notes, criticized her handwriting, and suggested she take a course in calligraphy. "An artist must strive for beauty in all things, Sergeant, even in constabulary affairs." He strode to the kitchen, shoulders slouched.

"Egad, what's this?" Holding the dripping paper bag between the tips of two fingers, Inspector Noserag dropped the squashed sandwiches into the garbage pail. "Remove your hat, Sergeant Kod; I am taking you to lunch."

Dickory stored the sleuths' hats on a closet shelf and followed Garson out of the house. Had she now been sent for sandwiches, she would have ordered him a ham and cheese.

Garson ordered a hamburger with everything on it and a Coke. An unusual choice, Dickory thought, for a slick society portrait painter, or the greatest detective in the universe who had yet to solve a case. Or the brooding employer who now sat opposite her. They ate in silence and walked back in silence. As they turned the bend into their narrow street, a man in dark glasses approached them. At first glance Dickory thought Manny Mallomar had another visitor, but then she noticed the tin cup, the tapping white cane, the German shepherd on a short lead.

Garson smiled at him! He smiled and bowed a sweeping bow and tossed a pebble into the blind man's cup.

Dickory frowned. The dog growled.

"Bless you," said the blind man.

Digging in her purse for change, Dickory wondered how Garson could be so kind to a hideous deaf-mute yet so callous toward a blind man. She dropped a quarter into his cup.

"We have company," Garson said flatly, pointing ahead.

Cobble Lane was a sea of staring faces. From the chief's car parked on the curb, the policeman-chauffeur stared at the derelict on the stoop. The derelict stared at the three women in the back seat. The three women, blonde, redhead, and brunette, stared at Shrimps Marinara, who was peering through the bedroom window at the policeman-chauffeur. From the basement window Isaac Bickerstaffe stared, just stared, and between the blinds on the second floor Chief Quinn's cigar bobbed up and down.

Manny Mallomar, who had let the chief of detectives into the house, leaned out of his door as they entered the hallway. Narrowing his bulging eyes, he shook a fat fist at Garson. In reply, Garson and Dickory bounded up the stairs with more noise than usual.

"Hickory Dickory Dock,
The mouse ran up the clock,
The clock struck two,
And up he flew,
Just like Hickory Dickory Dock.

"I just made that up," Chief Quinn said, pleased with himself.

"Sorry I'm late," Garson replied. "Let's get down to business."

2

"The Case of the Horrible Hairdresser," the chief announced dramatically after sitting down in the most comfortable chair and relighting the stub of his cigar. "The perpetrator works out of beauty parlors just long enough to get into some widow's confidence."

"Aha, the old confidence game," Garson exclaimed.

"May I continue?" the chief asked. Garson waved his permission. "The perpetrator sets the widow's hair a few times, then tells her he can make her ravishingly beautiful with a special formula he has invented. But—his formula is a secret, and he can't use it in someone else's shop. So, the widow makes a private appointment, and the next week she goes to the hairdresser's hotel room (always a different hotel) and gets the works."

"The works?" Dickory asked, alarmed.

"The works: shampoo, set, manicure, whatever a hairdresser does."

Dickory eased back into her chair.

"The widow looks into the mirror," Quinn continued. "She *is* ravishingly beautiful, or so she thinks. And now the con begins. The hairdresser can't use his fabulous formula again, he says, not until he pays ten thousand dollars to some chemist or other. Meanwhile, he can't patent it or put it on the market. Of course, he could take the chemist to court, but that would take years. Well, you can figure out the rest. The widow doesn't have years to wait. The formula works, she knows that; she also knows it could make millions. So, she lends him the ten grand and becomes part owner of the formula."

"And that's the last the widow sees of her money," Garson guessed, "and the hairdresser."

Quinn nodded. "Not only that. Three days after the treatment each of the widows wakes up bald. Bald as a billiard ball."

Garson didn't seem especially thrilled at the prospect of interviewing three bald widows. "Might as well bring them up," he said unenthusiastically. "All three together."

"One at a time is how we usually do it," Quinn explained. "The victims can influence one another's testimony or start arguing, and then what do you have?"

"The truth," Garson replied, donning his costume.

In paint-smeared smock and French beret, Garson bowed to the three wigged widows. "Welcome, mesdames. It is indeed a pleasure having three such lovely ladies grace my humble atelier." He kissed their hands.

The women giggled; the chief snickered. Dickory

found this new role humiliating. Garson was acting out a tourist's idea of a bohemian painter.

"My, what an artistic place you have here," said the red-wigged widow, gazing up at the skylight.

"So this is Greenwich Village," the blonde said.

The brunette pointed to the manikin. "Would you just look at this big jockey doll? Have you ever seen anything so quaint?"

The suave artist escorted his chattering guests to the straight-backed chairs between the easels. "Permit me to say how truly sorry I was to learn of your misfortune. None but the basest of criminals could have committed such an outrage on three such charming women. Acting out of the noblest charity, you have not only lost your piggy banks, but have been brutalized to boot."

A tear trickled down the cheek of the blonde-wigged widow; the redhead blinked at the dashing painter with gratitude. No one at the police station had treated them with such sympathy and understanding. Garson, with all his fakery, was soothing the widows' pain.

"Poor mesdames, I know how difficult this will be for you, but we must now speak about that despicable hairdresser. It is the only way we can get your money back, so please try to remember all the details, trivial as they may seem. My apprentice will take notes from which I will later paint a portrait and which you may then have to verify."

The widows were agreeable. The questioning began.

Garson asked the widow in the brown wig about the size of the horrible hairdresser.

"Not very large," she replied. "I'd say about five-feet six-inches tall."

"More like five-ten," said the short widow in the red wig. "And slim."

41

"Francis was five-seven or -eight," said the blonde-wigged one.

Notebook on her lap, Dickory sighed at the widows' lack of observation as she wrote down the various heights.

Garson asked for the hairdresser's full name.

"Francis White."

"Francis Black."

"Francis Green."

Quinn's cigar looked like an exclamation point at the end of his "I told you so" smirk. Wanting no part in this unprofessional interrogation, he left the arguing group to roam about the studio floor.

"Now we're getting somewhere," Garson said weakly. "We all agree that the hairdresser's first name is Francis. And I'm sure we will soon agree about his size."

"It's difficult," the blonde apologized. "You see, most of the time I was sitting and Francis was standing behind me. We did most of our talking into the mirror."

"Aha!" Garson exclaimed. "Then we shall recreate the scene of the crimes."

The chief of detectives groaned from the library.

Garson rolled the mirror across the floor and placed it before the seated women as first he, then Dickory, stood behind them. The three widows agreed, on seeing them through the mirror, that Dickory came loser in size. Perhaps an inch taller. No, they had not noticed Francis' shoes.

Dickory wrote "five-seven, more or less."

"Slim," Garson said. "One of you said slim."

"I did," the redhead replied.

"Slim?" scoffed the bitter brunette, who had lost more of her savings than the others. "That crook was hippy, even pear-shaped."

"How could you tell he was hippy?" the redhead

argued. "My Francis always wore a white coat, like a druggist."

"And a baby-blue shirt and a lavender bow tie," added the blonde. "And I'd go along with slim. Small-boned, anyway, with fine, delicate hands."

"But he gave a brisk shampoo, my Francis did," the redhead said. "And a perfect manicure."

Even the brunette had to agree to that.

Garson's questions were coming more rapidly now: hair, complexion, identifying marks. The widows argued; Dickory wrote; and Chief Quinn went upstairs to use the bathroom.

"Just one more question," Garson said, interrogation over. "Could you describe Francis in just one word? His most outstanding or most memorable feature."

"Sympathetic," said the blonde.

"Gentle," said the redhead.

It was quite clear how the hairdresser had found out about the widows' bank accounts. They had probably told him their life stories, and more.

The brunette could not describe Francis in just one word. "If you find that louse, hang him," she said.

The widows gone, the chief gone, Garson, no longer the charming bohemian artist, tossed his beret and smock on the table, poured himself a drink, and sank into the comfortable chair. Inspector Noserag could not begin the portrait of the horrible hairdresser until the new art supplies were delivered, and the society painter's portrait of the lawyer was finished and being framed. Bereft of roles to play, Garson's face once again became a blank mask.

"It's six o'clock," Dickory said, prepared to leave. She had completed her first week's work, but Garson's only response was a tired wave of his shaking hand. She decided to sing her request:

" 'Oranges and lemons,'
    say the bells of St. Clements;
'You owe me five farthings,'
    say the bells of St. Martins;
'When will you pay me?'
    say the bells of. . . .''

"Don't!" Garson leaped from his chair, spilling his drink. "Don't ever sing that song in this house again."

"I was just trying to hint about my pay."

"Oh." The artist walked to his desk. "I'm so sorry, Dickory, about shouting, and forgetting your money. I have a lot on my mind these days." This was not the phony Garson, who spoke so softly, nor was it the play-acting Garson. This was the Garson who cared for Isaac Bickerstaffe. This was the Kind One.

"Now, let's see," he said, scribbling figures on his desk pad. "Three hours a day for five days is fifteen, plus eight hours today makes twenty-three, times five dollars an hour makes one hundred fifteen."

The notice had mentioned "good pay," but this was extravagant for part-time work. Dickory did not complain.

"I'll have to give you a check."

Again she did not complain, although she had hoped to buy a book on her way home.

Garson, the mind reader, scanned his bookshelves and took down an expensive volume of full-color reproductions, the paintings of Piero della Francesca. "Here, take this. It's a bonus for hazardous duty, like getting sandwiches squashed."

3

Professor D'Arches paraded before the reworked monochromatic compositions and frowned. "Who's Dick Ory?"

Again she corrected him.

"Do you know what you've done here, Dickory?"

"I applied glazes to make dark tones." Dickory's glazes
consisted of double and triple applications of Magic
Markers over her original strokes. She had wanted to buy
real watercolors, but none of the stores would cash the
large check, and banks were closed on weekends.

"For your information, tones are light, shades are
dark. And glazes, yet!" The professor snorted, but the
students seemed impressed. Especially George III.

D'Arches snorted again before Harold Silverfish's
collage of pasted strips of foil. "Reynolds Wrap is not a

color," he shouted, then lowered his voice to a patronizing tone. "I assumed any student accepted into this school knew something about color or design, but I was wrong. Why should I expect anyone to appreciate good design today, what with the eye so consistently bombarded by bad examples, atrocious examples of incompetent graphic art, everywhere, at home, in the streets—those awful signs in the streets." D'Arches paused to control his soaring emotions. "Let's begin again. Forget design this time; concentrate only on color, one color. Everyone arrange their tones and shades in triangles within a square as Dick Ory has done."

Basking in the success of having her design selected, Dickory missed most of the professor's parting sentence. All she heard were the last three words: Roy G. Biv!

"What did he say about Roy G. Biv?" she asked Harold Silverfish, grabbing him by the sleeve as he was about to leave the classroom.

"He said everybody's got to confine himself to the spectrum. No more silver foil, just stick to Roy G. Biv."

What in the world did that mean: stick to Roy G. Biv. Dickory had looked up "Biv" in every reference book in the school library but had found nothing. "Who is Roy G. Biv?"

Harold Silverfish shrugged. "Never heard of him."

"I know," George III said, shining with enthusiasm. "I'll tell you about Roy G. Biv, if you tell me how you get such a gloss on your watercolors."

"How do you know about Roy G. Biv?"

"Oh, we learned about it in the fifth grade."

Dickory looked into the wide-eyed, freckled face, wondering what outer-space cornfield he came from. "I use Magic Markers," she admitted quickly.

"Really? That's amazing. Golly, I wish I had your nerve."

"Please, George, I'm in a big hurry. Who's Roy G. Biv?"

"Not who, what. Roy G. Biv's not a person." George chuckled good-naturedly. "Roy G. Biv is an acronym; you know, when initials spell out a name. The letters ROYGBIV stand for the colors of the spectrum, in order, like in a rainbow: Red, Orange, Yellow, Green, Blue, Indigo, Violet. Roy G. Biv—it's an easy way to remember them."

Troubled with questions, unaskable questions, Dickory hurried to her job. The paints in the second taboret were kept in the order of the spectrum, that's what Garson had meant when he said Roy G. Biv. Then who was the messy artist who painted so furiously? And why was his canvas hidden under a velvet drape?

Turning the bend into Cobble Lane, Dickory almost bumped into the blind man. He quickly stepped aside.

A truck pulled up to the curb as Dickory was about to enter Number 12. Mallomar peered through a crack in his door and shut it when he saw the size of the men who carried the art supplies up the stairs to the studio.

Garson was not home. Roy G. Biv (or whatever his name was) had not been working. The messy taboret was clean; his easel was undraped and empty; the manikin stood naked of jockey silks. Dickory unpacked the acrylic paints and stored them in the drawers of the new taboret in the order of the spectrum: red, orange, yellow, green, blue. . . .

The doorbell rang.

"I wanna she Garshon," the derelict slurred. This was a different bum from his Bowery brother who usually slept on the stoop across the street. "Whershz Garshon?" He pushed past Dickory, staggered drunkenly down the hall, and lurched up the stairs. His long gray hair was un-combed (a wig?). His unshaven face was covered (disguised?) with dirt. He wore an eye patch (!) and a torn work shirt tucked into shrunken pants (!!) .

"The new art supplies are here," Dickory said to the derelict's back.

Garson stopped in the middle of the stairs, turned and raised his eye patch. "What gave me away?"

"One blue eye. Trim waist."

"Oh," was all he said.

Showered and shaved, fresh for the detective game, Garson came down to the studio dressed in his usual costume: starched white shirt with sleeves rolled high on his arms, tailored blue jeans, loafers. On his head was the deerstalker hat. He said nothing about his derelict disguise, and Dickory had learned not to ask questions.

"Okay, Kod, get the notebook. We got no time to lose." He handed Dickory the bobby's helmet, slumped down in the wing chair, curled his upper lip tight against his teeth, crossed his legs, uncrossed them, folded his arms, unfolded them, clasped his hands behind his head, then brought them down and joined them around one knee. Garson was still experimenting with his new role.

Dickory read loud from her revised notes. "The Case of the Horrible Hairdresser. Name of perpetrator: Francis aka. . . ."

"What does 'aka' mean?" asked the greatest sleuth in the universe, Inspector Noserag.

" 'Aka' means 'also known as,' " Dickory explained.

"Good thinking, Sergeant Kod. Go on."

"Name of perpetrator: Francis.
    aka: Francis White, Francis Black, Francis Green.
  Occupation: Hairdresser. Cuts, sets, combs hair.
    Gives brisk shampoos and perfect manicures.

Height: five-seven, more or less.
Size: slim / hippy, pear-shaped / small-boned.
Hands: delicate.
Hair color: red / golden-red / strawberry blond.
Hair style: crew cut / very short / just short.
Skin: fair / creamy / smooth.
Identifying marks: small mole on lower right cheek.
Clothes: white druggist's coat, baby-blue shirt, lavender bow tie.
Comments: sympathetic / gentle / louse."

Inspector Noserag's "hmmm" was followed by several minutes of silence. "Do we possess the correct costumes for attiring our manikin, Sergeant Kod?"

"We have a white doctor's coat, but no baby-blue shirt or lavender bow tie," Dickory replied.

"Bah, ridiculous fashion colors. I shall borrow a shirt and bow tie from my good friend Garson and paint in the correct colors—what would they be? Cerulean blue, perhaps, and cobalt violet light. Lucky thing Francis always wore the same clothes, or I'd be painting a portrait of a man with three ties. Hmmm, that's interesting."

"What?"

"I think we may have a clue here."

"Where?"

"Questions, questions. Please, no more questions." Inspector Noserag parroted his good friend Garson, then lapsed into silence again. "Hmmm. Sergeant Kod, what I need is a pipe. Quick, find me a pipe. A detective cannot detect without a pipe."

Deciding not to mention that the chief of detectives smoked cigars, Dickory selected a long-stemmed pipe with a curved bowl from the costume collection.

"Excellent. Now, Sergeant, if you would be good

enough to dash over to the tobacconist's, I will encostume our figgers appropri'tly."

"What did Sherlock Holmes smoke in his pipe?" Dickory asked the knowledgeable owner of the Village Smoke Shop.

"Shag," he replied. "What are you, some sort of freaky cop in disguise?"

Realizing with horror that she was still wearing the bobby's helmet, Dickory reached for the nearest pouch of pipe tobacco, tossed the correct change on the counter, and stalked out of the shop in a huff of indignation.

The tobacco smelled like tooth decay, but the inspector didn't seem to mind. He puffed away and contemplated the costumed manikins. One, in flowered housedress and yellow wig, was seated before the tall mirror. Behind the dummy widow stood the dummy hairdresser, faceless and hairless, wearing a white shirt, a polka-dot bow tie, and a doctor's coat. Noserag bent the segmented arms at the elbows and twined a strand of the customer's hair around its wedge-shaped hands.

"Ready with the palette, Sergeant Kod?"

Dickory had been told to arrange the paints for the portrait, not according to Roy G. Biv this time, but in the sequence in which they appeared in the descriptions. "I wasn't sure about the flesh tones," she said, handing the glass palette to the painter.

Inspector Noserag puffed on his pipe and puzzled over her choice of colors. "These don't seem to be in order. Let's see: white for the jacket; black for the . . . oh, yes, black for the mole; chromium oxide green for the. . . . What's the green for?"

The colors were in correct order, but in her haste Dickory had included Francis' three last names.

"You've got a lot to learn, kid, a lot to learn," Noserag muttered in Bogart's voice.

Not one to take criticism lightly, Dickory quickly invented a reason for her mistake. "You are quite right, Inspector, I do have a lot to learn; but if you look carefully you will see that my color selection may be a clue to the hairdresser's present alias. Francis Black, White, Green; why not Francis Blue, Francis Gold, Francis Brown, or Francis Gray?"

"Precisely," Inspector Noserag replied. "I was wondering just how long it would take you to uncover that clue, Sergeant. As I always say, where there's a crime, there's a pattern."

Garson was bluffing. His earlier hint of a clue had to do with the colors of the shirt and tie. "Yes, there is a pattern," Dickory replied, "as you always say."

Brush poised, Garson studied the manikins, puffed on his pipe, turned and studied their mirrored images, and puffed and puffed on his noxious pipe. At last he dipped the tip of his brush into the black paint and raised it to the canvas.

Dickory had her own picture of the hairdresser well-drawn in her mind, but it in no way resembled what Garson painted.

"Aha!" he exclaimed. He looked in the mirror at his finished portrait, lay down his brush, and smiled triumphantly. "Inspector Noserag has solved the case!"

Puzzled, Dickory stared at his canvas. The portrait of the horrible hairdresser consisted of one small black dot. And then the inspector said what she had known he would say sooner or later.

"Elementary, my dear Kod, elementary."

4

Her helmet removed, Dickory was still puzzling over the black dot on the otherwise blank canvas when the chief of detectives rushed in. He was too busy today for nursery rhymes.

"I'm a very busy man, Garson. This is not my only case, you know." Quinn refused to sit down. "What in heaven's name couldn't you tell me over the phone?"

Garson was in no hurry to reply. He wanted to savor his first sweet triumph as a detective. "How many ties do you own, Chief?"

Today Quinn was wearing a navy blue tie with a fine red stripe. It was a nice tie, tastefully chosen. So were his clothes, or what could be seen of them beneath the cigar ash. Dickory guessed that his wife selected his wardrobe for him.

"How should I know how many ties I own?" Quinn grumbled. "You think that's all I have to do is count my ties? Fifteen, maybe twenty; what's the difference? If you must know, ask my wife; she picks out my clothes."

Pleased with her deduction, Dickory turned away to hide her smile.

"And how many police officers wear long sideburns?" Garson asked.

The chief fingered a sideburn that stopped just short of his earlobe. "These aren't long; no longer than anybody else's these days. You should see some of my street detectives; one of them even wears a ponytail. Why, you got a complaint about hairy cops or something?" Quinn stopped his anxious pacing before the black-dot painting and almost swallowed his cigar stub. "So this is your portrait of the perpetrator. No wonder you couldn't describe it over the phone. What did you paint it with, invisible ink?"

"That is not a portrait," Garson replied evenly, "it is the solution. Let me lead you step by step, clue by clue, to the indisputable result of my astounding logic."

"Just get to the point, Garson. Do you know where to find the hairdresser, or don't you?"

Garson sighed. "The hairdresser is either still working the con game or, having made enough money to go straight, now owns a beauty shop."

"Brilliant." Quinn raised his eyes to the skylight in prayer for salvation from such fools.

Ignoring the sarcasm, Garson continued. "Now, listen carefully, Chief. The perpetrator is now using a name of a different color, like Francis Brown or Francis Gray. And the mole is on the left cheek, not the right. Oh, and one more thing, if she is using her real name, Frances will be spelled with an *e*."

"She?" both the chief and Dickory exclaimed.

"That's right," Garson replied. "The horrible hairdresser is a woman."

The chief's sudden exit brought the curtain down in the middle of Garson's dramatic monologue. He slouched in his chair, a pose of disappointment and defeat. His hand shook.

"That was an amazing feat of deduction, Inspector Noserag," Dickory said, placing the deerstalker hat on his head. "It may seem elementary to you, but I still don't know how you did it."

Garson rose, poured himself a drink, lit his pipe and, eyes twinkling, was once again transformed into the inspector. "Ah, yes, The Case of the Horrible Hairdresser," he said meditatively. "One of my most difficult and intriguing puzzlements, and perhaps my most brilliant success. You remember, Sergeant Kod, my original misgivings about the sky-blue shirt and lavender bow tie. Those atrocious colors provided me with my first clue: each witness reported the identical attire. Now, there is something quite odd about a man who owns but one necktie. I, myself, wouldn't be caught dead wearing a tie, unless I were applying for a bank loan or facing a jury, yet there must be twenty-five ties hanging in my closet." He meant Garson's closet.

"I see," Dickory replied. "One bow tie—a woman's disguise."

"Precisely, Sergeant. A bow tie is hardly a proper disguise for a man. The second clue was the hair: crew cut / very short / just short. The hairdresser's hair was growing, no disguise there, but why would a man in this day and age, especially a man in that profession, wear his hair so unfashionably short? My deduction: because long hair would look ridiculous with no sideburns."

"Maybe he went bald trying out his own formula," Dickory offered, "and his hair was just growing in again."

"I thought of that, Sergeant Kod, and it is very likely the case. But if he were a man he would have worn a wig until his hair grew back. After all, he would not have lost his facial hair."

"Skin disease?" Dickory guessed weakly.

Noserag shook his head. "Skin: smooth, creamy. No, my con man is a con woman who, naturally enough, could not grow a beard, and hence, could not grow sideburns."

"Very good, Inspector."

Inspector Noserag blew a smoke ring before continuing. "The third clue was the perfect manicure. Never, in my long and illustrious career of investigating human foibles, have I heard of a male manicurist. Have you?"

Dickory sat on her hands to hide their ragged cuticles. "No."

"One bow tie, no sideburns, perfect manicures. I had no doubt, no doubt whatever, that I was dealing with a dashingly clever and dangerous woman. Eureka, I said to myself. . . ."

"What about the mole?" Dickory was tiring of the ham acting. "All three widows agreed that the mole was on Frances' right cheek, but you said left cheek."

"And so I did, so I did. I immediately rejected the notion that the mole was anything but real. Not only was it raised, but it is a most difficult feat of disguise to paste a mole always in exactly the same spot. As for being on the right cheek, come with me, Sergeant."

Noserag removed the manikin in the housedress and placed Dickory in the chair before the mirror. "Now tell me, Sergeant Kod, on what cheek is the mole?"

For the first time Dickory noticed that Garson had

painted a black spot, not only on his canvas, but on the face of the hairdresser dummy. "On the right cheek," she said, looking into the mirror. Then she turned to the wooden Frances behind her. "I mean the left cheek." She, too, had been confused by the mirror's reversed image. "Brilliant, Inspector Noserag."

"Thank you, Sergeant Kod."

The Case of the
Face on the Five-Dollar Bill

1

Dickory had fallen in love with the paintings of Piero della Francesca; even more, she had fallen in love with herself as one of his haunted angels. Unlike the usual flying Kewpie dolls, Piero's angels stood tall in a calm and noble beauty. Feet planted solidly on earth, their eyes stared dreamily upon unimaginable visions of heaven.

Only the blind man seemed unaware of the wingless angel that floated into Cobble Lane that afternoon. Head held high, eyes focused on inward beauty, Dickory entered the house oblivious to the sodden sins of the sprawling drunk on the stoop and the fleshy excess of Manny Mallomar. Had Shrimps been in the hall at that moment, he would have been crunched under the tread of the visiting angel whose one mighty stride could rid the world of all pestilence and vermin forever.

"Hey, brat. No more asking my visitors' names, you hear?" Mallomar yelled from his doorway. "Did you hear me, you lousy snoop?"

She did not hear. The angel wafted up the stairs, ears sealed to secular profanities.

"Have you heard anything I said, Dickory?" Garson asked, having explained the workings of the slide projector to his glassy-eyed apprentice for the second time. "You're not on drugs, are you?"

"No," she replied dreamily.

"Then answer the front door. The bell has rung twice already."

It was impossible to be an unearthly angel face-to-face with an earthly jellybean like Mrs. Julius B. Panzpresser.

"Just call me Cookie," she said, bursting with cheerfulness right out of the seams of her shocking-pink pants suit. "And what is your name, pretty one?"

"Dick. . . ." She stopped short. If ever Dickory had seen a nursery-rhyme spouter, this was she.

"Dick?" Cookie Panzpresser exclaimed. "How very unusual; but it's better than Kimberly; everybody I know has a grandchild named Kimberly; never even heard that name when I was growing up; I have six myself, not Kimberlys, grandchildren: there's Susie, she's the oldest, then there's Jason and. . . ."

Manny Mallomar was so bored he closed his door.

"The studio is upstairs, Mrs. Panzpresser," Dickory said after the list of grandchildren was completed.

"Cookie. Everyone calls me Cookie." Cookie jogged up the stairs, her bleached-blonde hair becoming more tousled with each plump bounce. At the top she leaned against the door frame, panting. Garson, wearing his blue silk turtleneck and dirty jeans, led his client to the wing chair.

"The years are catching up with little Cookie." She gasped, plopped down, and fanned herself with his mail.

"You don't look a day over thirty-five," Garson said, his voice dripping with charm.

"None of that, you big fraud," Cookie replied. "If you're going to lie, lie with your paintbrush, not with your mouth." Her remark was delivered with such good humor that Garson let her prattle on while he searched her face for the lost youthfulness he would restore in her portrait.

"Did you have a chance to meet the Big Cigar at my dinner party the other night? That's what I call him; his real name is Chief of Detectives Joe Quinn. Julius, that's my husband, asked him to help find a missing artist."

"Who's missing?" Dickory asked.

"Edward Sonnenblum, or something like that. There's only one painting by him in the whole world—Julius owns that one, but he wants another one. Julius has had a private detective looking for the artist for years, but he quit."

"Now about your portrait, Cookie," Garson said abruptly.

"Oh, yes, my portrait. It's for Julius, for his birthday, to add to his collection, you know. It's going to be a surprise."

Dickory pictured the art collector's surprise at receiving a Garson painting. Horror was a better word. But Garson reacted as though his paintings did, indeed, belong among the greats. "A splendid idea, Cookie; and you will be a splendid subject. I don't have any portraits to show you, you understand—they are all in their happy owners' hands—but I can show you slides to give you an idea of pose and dress. My assistant, Ms. Dock, will. . . ."

"Dock? I thought she said 'Dick.' "

There was no way out of it. "Dickory Dock," said Dickory Dock.

"Dickory Dock? How cheerful," Mrs. Panzpresser exclaimed. "Let's see, now, how does that go?

> "Hickory Dickory Dock,
> The mouse ran up the clock,
> The clock struck one,
> And down he come. . . .

"One—come; that doesn't rhyme, does it?"

Garson quickly drew the blinds and raised the screen. Dickory turned on the slide projector and read from a list of sitters' names with each corresponding click. Cookie Panzpresser oohed and aahed and burbled about how much younger and handsomer her friends looked in their portraits.

"Mrs. Juanita Chiquita Dobson," Dickory read.

"Next!" Garson shouted, and she clicked to the next slide before Cookie had a chance to study the banana heiress' portrait.

"That was one of my first attempts and not up to my standards," Garson explained. "Now, here is my most recent painting; I think you are acquainted with my lawyer."

"That's too good for the old slob," Mrs. Julius B. Panzpresser remarked, but when the next slide flashed she cheered. "That's what I want my picture to look like. That's just how Julius would like me to look, like a lady pouring tea."

Cookie wanted Garson to begin her portrait right away, but she had to juggle club dates and charity functions to find time for the preliminary sitting. "Ta-ta, everybody," she sang, bouncing down the stairs. "I've got to run and get my hair done for tonight's benefit."

"One minute, Cookie," Garson called after her. "Your hairdresser's name isn't Francis, is it?"

"No, Antoine. Why?"

"Nothing. Have a nice evening."

2

Dickory left with a shopping bag full of half-used tubes of oil paint left over from the lawyer's portrait, four slightly frayed brushes, and the large, stretched canvas with the small black dot. "Get rid of them for me," Garson had said.

Arms loaded with bounty, Dickory could barely maneuver through the front door, especially with Shrimps Marinara trying to enter at the same time.

"Out of my way, punk," he growled when the canvas brushed against his drooping overcoat.

Shrimps did not like to be touched.

No matter, neither did the Piero della Francesca angel.

"What a stink," her brother complained. He was stretched out on the living room sofa (Dickory's bed), watching television. "Somebody open a window."

Dickory swished her paintbrush in the offensive turpentine, opened a window, and returned to her painting.

"Somebody close the window, quick," shouted her sister-in-law Blanche, bent over the ironing board. "The dirt's flying all over my clean uniform."

"Back and forth, back and forth," Dickory muttered in imitation of her brother as she closed the window. Once again she picked up her brush and contemplated the canvas propped against the wall. Her composition consisted of a single object balanced against a mass. If done right, the eye will always come to rest on the isolated object, Professor D'Arches had explained. She was working on the mass, covering the entire bottom third of the canvas with blocks of overlapping color, thinking out each brushstroke carefully so that no one color would pop out more than the others. Now she knew why Garson wanted a quiet assistant; even painting a mass of colors in oils took intense concentration.

"And just what do you know about back and forth, Miss Pablo Picasso?" her brother asked. "Maybe if someone had supported me when I was your age, I'd be doing something better than driving a bus back and forth, back and forth."

"I pay my way," Dickory replied. In generosity she did not mention that her brother had lost the hock shop to his bookie; but then, she had lied about her salary, telling them the twenty dollars a week she paid for room and board was half of her wages. She was saving her money to move out of this crummy walk-up railroad flat. She wanted her own crummy walk-up studio, all to herself. She wanted to become an important artist—or would she rather be a rich hack artist, like Garson, and live and work in a fine house?

"Well, I'll say this," Blanche said, ironing ruffles on her nurse's cap. "I'd rather be driving back and forth, back and forth, than doing what I'm doing. How'd you like to be drooled on by senile great-grandfathers?"

"Yeah," Donald argued. "Yeah, well I'll give you just one day driving back and forth, back and forth. . . ."

Professor D'Arches brushed the back of his hand over the expensive linen canvas, thick with pure oil pigments. "What did you do, Dickory, rob a bank?" That was all he had to say about her single object versus mass. He spent the rest of the period castigating the cluttered, poorly designed street signs.

"I thought your composition was really fantastic," George III said, trying to slow his long-legged stride to the angel's serene pace. "The mass of color was really good, and the single object—that was a stroke of genius. Just one little black dot."

"Thank you, George. I found your design quite original, too," she replied with heavenly charity. "Imagine, balancing a watermelon on top of a pea."

"Wow, is this where you live?" They had reached Number 12. "Is that your father in the window?"

Dickory uttered a haughty laugh. "Of course not, that's our janitor."

"Really?" Even gullible George was incredulous. "That fat man in white, your janitor?"

Dickory was about to explain that they had very clean garbage when Shrimps appeared next to Mallomar. "That little man in black is our janitor; the fat one in the white suit is our cook."

Pleased that the derelict was not around to spoil the

elegance of Cobble Lane, Dickory unlocked the door to her house, leaving George on the sidewalk gawking at her wealth.

"Who's the character outside, the one eyeing the joint?" Mallomar's questions always sounded like threats.

Head held high, Dickory floated through the hall in an aura of silent sanctity.

"I'm talking to you, you snotty kid; and I'm expecting an answer." The angry fat man spun her around and grabbed her nose between two greasy knuckles.

Dickory kicked him in the shins and escaped up the stairs, praying that the steep flight was too great a challenge to Mallomar's corpulence.

It was. "I'll get you, if you don't stop that snooping. Just you wait." From the bottom of the stairs he shook a white-knuckled fist at her.

"Get stuck in the bathtub, you fat greaseball," the Piero della Francesca angel shouted down. "You fat black-mailer, you."

Mallomar's bulging eyes glared. Dickory glared back, realizing the truth of what she had said. He *was* a black-mailer. He was blackmailing the Smiths and the Joneses. And Garson.

Dickory tore herself away from the ugliness below and walked into the studio, caressing her sore nose. What did Mallomar have on Garson? What dark crime blackened Garson's past? No questions, no questions; she couldn't ask Garson or dare touch on the subject even if he had been home.

"Garson?" she called. No answer. She looked out of the front window. No one was in Cobble Lane, just George still gaping. He saw her, smiled brightly, waved, and walked away.

Maybe she should quit this job, in spite of the good

pay. It wasn't the ugly tenants or the blackmail that troubled Dickory as much as what she was learning from Garson. She was learning to be a phony.

The canvas on Garson's easel told the beginnings of the Cookie Panzpresser portrait, the underpainting already shaping the dignity of the sitter.

The second easel was again draped. Next to it sat a manikin dressed as a drum majorette, a plumed hat atilt on its blonde curly wig.

"Garson?" Dickory called again to make certain he was not around. Cautiously, she lifted a corner of the red velvet drape and nearly jumped out of her sneakers when the doorbell rang. Deciding to let Mr. Smith or Mrs. Jones wait, she raised the drape.

The canvas was primed, but unpainted. Blank.

Disappointed that her transgression had led to nothing but a nervous sweat, Dickory ran down the stairs to answer the insistent bell. The suspicious Shrimps peeked into the hallway, reminding her of her sore nose. She opened the front door.

"I'm sorry, Garson isn't home," she said, on hearing that the crippled man's name was Fetlock.

"I will wait, thank you." Fetlock spoke in a high, piping voice. His hair was black. His eyes were hidden under bushy brows. His bent body was disguised by a long, collared cape. One boot had a sole three inches thicker than the other. Slowly, painfully, he dragged his deformed leg up the steps, his left hand clutching the banister, his right hand quivering on a gold-handled cane.

"I see you've begun the Cookie Panzpresser portrait, Mr. Fetlock," Dickory said to his crooked back.

The bent man straightened. "How did you know it was me?"

"The tremor in your right hand."

Garson banged his cane against the wall and stormed up the stairs as best he could in the uneven boots.

It was no longer just a game. What was it then, she wondered as she slowly climbed the stairs. Why was Garson testing disguises?

Again the doorbell rang.

"Hello, Chief Quinn," Dickory announced loudly toward the crack in Mallomar's door.

"Hello, Hickory. Garson in?"

"Come on up, Chief," Garson called. Disguise discarded, he looked like the portrait painter again, except for his bare feet. He had not had time to find his loafers. "Did you find the horrible hairdresser?"

"Sure did," Quinn replied cheerfully, sitting on the desktop next to the telephone. "Frances was ensconced in the premises of her new beauty parlor."

"Her?"

"All right, I thank you and pat you on the back. The hairdresser is a woman with a mole on her left cheek. The only place you went wrong is her last name: Ocher."

"Ocher *is* a color," Dickory insisted.

"An earth color," Garson said. "Tell me, did the widows get their money back?"

"Not yet, but they're happy with the arrangement. Frances Ocher bought a beauty shop with their money, so the widows settled for a percentage of the profits and free hair sets in perpetuity. Of course, the formula will be destroyed." The chief sighed. "Victims of their own vanity." He shook his head philosophically and removed the cigar for his next serious pronouncement. "Vanity, greed, jealousy, hatred—eliminate them and you eliminate three-quarters of all offenses. Vanity. Greed. Jealousy. Hatred. The four horsemen of modern crime."

A phone call interrupted the Quinn theory of the criminal mind. "Yeah, he's here," the chief mumbled angrily, cigar back in his mouth. Dickory thought she heard the caller whine something about one entrance and Jim. Quinn's cigar danced crazily. "Okay, come on back; but you lose him once more and you'll be directing traffic in the Lincoln Tunnel." He slammed the receiver, eased himself into the wing chair, and stared at Dickory. The smile returned to his ruddy face.

"Hickory Dickory Dock,
    The mouse ran up the clock,
        The clock struck three,
        The mouse did flee,
    Hickory Dickory Dock."

Dickory turned away.

"Come on, Hickory Dickory Dock, don't be sore," Quinn said. "Not everyone can make people happy just by telling them their name."

Dickory Dock was a name for a tap-dancing, curly-haired tot, she thought. And it certainly did not make her happy.

"After all, it's not really a funny name." Chief Quinn would not give up. "It's not a funny name like Wyatt Earp. I always thought Wyatt Earp sounded more like a belch than a name. You've got to be tough with a name like that one."

Dickory thought of her tough brother Donald, who beat up anyone who dared quack at him.

"Speaking of names," Quinn said, "what do you make of this one: Eldon F. Zyzyskczuk?"

Dickory shrugged. It was an unusual name, but not especially funny. "How do you spell it?"

"Exactly the way it sounds." The chief burst out laughing at his little joke.

"You know what I think about that name?" Garson had returned wearing shoes. "I think there must be one, and only one, Eldon F. Zyzyskczuk."

"I knew you'd say that, Garson, but this time you are wrong. There happens to be not one, but two Eldon F. Zyzyskczuks. Two Eldon Feodor Zyzyskczuks," the chief repeated. "One's an importer, who lives at 734 West 84th Street; the other's an exporter, who lives at 743 East 84th Street. A few years back the importer lost his wallet and sent away for a new Social Security card; now both Eldon F. Zyzyskczuks have the same Social Security number." Quinn chuckled over the unhappy plight of the tax authorities, two banks, five department stores, and six credit-card companies, none of whom could collect on their mixed-up bills.

"I hope you're not asking me to paint a double portrait of the two Eldon F. Zyzyskczuks," Garson said.

"No, no, there's no crime involved here. It's just one big, beautiful mess, and thank heavens the police are not involved." Quinn rose and withdrew an envelope thick with money from his pocket. "But I would like your help on another case. The feds are in on this one, and I'd like to wrap it up before they do." He handed a bill to Garson. "And here's one for you, Hickory. Don't spend it all in one place."

Dickory studied the Lincoln Memorial on her bill. The color looked right; the paper felt right; the engraving looked right; but the police would not be passing real money around. She turned over the counterfeit bill and gasped at what she saw.

A car horn honked twice.

"Let me know what you make of that portrait, Garson. By telephone this time, if you please." The chief headed for the door. "Oh, by the way, I call this one: The Case of the Face on the Five-Dollar Bill."

3

"Has he gone?" Garson asked, examining the counter-feiter's portrait on the five-dollar bill.

Dickory checked the window. Quinn seemed to be warning the derelict, rather angrily, it seemed. His words were obviously wasted, for as soon as the chief's car disappeared around the bend, the drunk returned to his stoop and went to sleep.

Out came the hats. Inspector Noserag lit his pipe and leaned back in his chair. "A most intriguing case, Sergeant Kod, most intriguing. What is your learned opinion of my fellow-artist who usurped Lincoln's oval?"

Dickory tried to forget about the derelict and concentrate on the counterfeiter's face on her counterfeit bill. "He must want to get caught."

"Not necessarily, Sargeant. Examine the face carefully and describe it to me."

There was little to describe. "Ordinary," Dickory replied with a shrug.

"Handsome?"

"Maybe. In an ordinary sort of way."

"Precisely. My counterfeiter could pass these bills for a lifetime without being apprehended. Cashiers cannot examine each and every five-dollar bill that passes through their hands. By the time they discover that the bill is counterfeit, they cannot remember who passed it. And if some of them did remember, 'Ordinary,' they would say. And if they saw him again, would they recognize him? 'I doubt it,' they would say. 'He looked just like anybody else. Ordinary.' "

"But the counterfeiter's face is right here," Dickory argued. "Anyone can see exactly what he looks like."

"Remember, Sergeant Kod, this is a portrait, not a photograph. Would you recognize my lawyer in the flesh from the man in the portrait? I think not. We are dealing here with one of Quinn's four horsemen: vanity." Garson, aware of Inspector Noserag's lapse in character, coughed and changed his British to Bogart. "Any guy who plasters his mug on a phony five-spot has got to be vain. Get the palette ready, kid. Inspector Noserag is going to paint from handsome to real."

"Your palette, Inspector." Dickory placed a pen and a bottle of India ink on the taboret top and smirked.

Eyebrows raised, Noserag looked from the "palette" to the black-and-white portrait on the engraved bill. "Quite right, Sergeant, I shall draw this likeness in pen and ink. But what is this? Can it be possible? Eureka!" The bill fluttered in his shaking hand. "Quick, Sergeant Kod, my glass."

Dickory hastened to the kitchen counter to pour him a drink.

"Not a drinking glass, a glass!" the inspector shouted. "My magnifying lens. In the desk. Never mind, I'll get it myself. Look at your bill, Sergeant. Does it also have a thumbprint on it—a red, smudged thumbprint?"

It did.

"Aha," he exclaimed, examining both bills under the lens. "Unquestionably this is the thumbprint of my counterfeiter."

"How do you know it belongs to the counterfeiter?"

"Elementary, my dear Kod. The exact print appears on two different bills. I dare say, the police would not leave their own thumbprints on the evidence, at least not red ones."

"Well, one thumbprint isn't much help," Dickory said. "The police need a complete set of fingerprints, and and even those can't be traced unless they have a record of original prints for comparison."

"I was quite aware of that, Sergeant," the inspector replied huffily.

You were not, thought Sergeant Kod.

Resuming his chair, Inspector Noserag puffed on his pipe and closed his eyes to show that he was thinking. The portrait painting postponed, Dickory took up her notebook and awaited the results of the great detective's deliberations.

At last he spoke. "The red smudged thumbprints tell us two things about my counterfeiter. One: he passed his bills face down, therefore he is cautious. Two: he is in working contact with some sort of red stain."

"Printer's ink?" Dickory guessed.

Noserag shook his head. "The bills are printed in black and green."

"He wasn't printing the bills when he was passing them. Maybe he was working on another job."

"Good thinking, Sergeant, but my counterfeiter has been passing these bills for months. If he had ink on his thumbs, why was it always red ink, and why only his thumbs? No, I propound that this is a stain of another origin."

Dickory knew better than to suggest to the proud inspector that they ask the police crime lab for help. She studied the red stain more closely. It looked familiar. She had seen a similar stain somewhere else.

"Pistachio nuts," she announced. Her brother Donald ate pistachio nuts while watching baseball games on television. Blanche was always yelling at him for missing the refuse bowl. By the time the game was over, the carpet would be strewn with shells, and Donald's thumbs would be red.

"Pistachio nuts," Noserag repeated, examining the thumbprints under his glass. "By gad, you're right; we are dealing with a pistachio-nut addict. Congratulations, Sergeant Kod."

"Elementary, my dear Noserag, elementary."

"Hmmm."

For a few uncomfortable minutes Garson stared at Dickory through narrowed slits. She turned away wondering if he was angered by her mockery or whether his eyes were irritated by the pipe smoke.

"Speaking of red, what happened to your nose?"

Dickory looked at herself in the tall mirror. Her nose was red, all right. "I ran into a door."

"A fat door wearing a white suit, I would surmise," he replied.

Dickory spun around, wondering how he had guessed.

"Rudimentary, my dear Kod, rudimentary."

The following afternoon Dickory discovered the reason for the large mirror in the artist's studio. Rigid as a frozen pork chop, Cookie Panzpresser sat posed before the mirror, hypnotized by her reflected image as a lady about to pour tea. Garson stood before his easel, a paintbrush in his hand, an eye patch over one eye.

"That will be all for today, Cookie," he said, taking the Rose Medallion teacup from her hand and breaking the spell.

A laughing, chattering Cookie came to life. "Oh, hello there, Dickory Dock, I didn't hear you come in. Isn't that clever, that eye patch? I never knew until Garson explained it to me that you need two eyes to see in three dimensions, and one eye for two dimensions. Garson is painting me with one eye in two dimensions, flat like Gauguin. Isn't that right?"

Garson did not respond. The nearly completed painting was highlighted and shadowed in three dimensions. It looked just like any other Garson portrait of a non-aging woman, the face smoothed of wrinkles, each hair in its shining place.

"Garson can also paint in one dimension," Dickory said, thinking of the hairdresser's one-dot portrait.

"Really? How clever. Well, I've got to get going or I'll be late for some committee meeting or other, I forget which. So long, Garson. And toodle-oo Miss Longface with the Cheery Name." Mrs. Panzpresser patted Dickory on the cheek and bounced out.

"Don't bother with that mess," Garson said.

Dickory was cleaning the cluttered taboret, capping tubes of Mars violet and vermilion—the colors of the drum majorette's costume. Garson lifted his eye patch, revealing a blackened eye. He must have protested Mallomar's nose-tweaking and run into the same fat, white door. "Thanks, Garson," Dickory said gratefully.

"Inspector Noserag to you," he replied, donning the deerstalker. "Now, let us resume our deliberations on The Case of the Face on the Five-Dollar Bill."

Garson rolled the mirror from the Cookie Panzpresser painting to the Noserag easel. Reaching with difficulty into the pocket of his tight jeans, he extracted an authentic five-dollar bill and tacked it to one corner of the blank canvas next to its counterfeit. "Read me what you got so far, kid." His voice was hard and tough, in keeping with his black eye.

Dickory read: "Counterfeiter: Male, Caucasian."

"Not bad, Sergeant. I hadn't thought of that. Go on."

"Ordinary features. Vain. Cautious. Addicted to pistachio nuts (red)."

Noserag dictated as he compared the five-dollar bills through his magnifying glass. "Professional engraver. Poor artist—no, change that to excellent draftsman. Here, Sergeant, look at the finely drawn lines on the borders. Not only are these lines not traced, but my man added some flourishes of his own."

"But the portrait is out of drawing," Dickory commented.

"You have a good eye, Sergeant. One of the features is most definitely not in proportion to the rest of the face; and that is our biggest clue yet."

"I don't understand."

"Which is why I am an inspector and you are still a sergeant," was the only explanation Garson had to offer. "And here's another clue. Look at the lines on the jacket over the second *n* in Lincoln. Compare them with these lines on the bogus bill."

Dickory had to hold Garson's hand to keep the magnifying glass from shaking. "The lines are angled in opposite directions," she said.

"Correct. Now, take the pen, dip it in the ink, and draw the lines as they appear on the real fiver, these lines here on Lincoln's jacket." Dickory stood before the blank canvas. Now her hand shook. "Go ahead, draw," he insisted.

Dickory drew three short, shy hatches slanting downward from left to right as they appeared on the authentic bill.

"Having trouble?" Garson asked.

"I'm not used to pen and ink."

Garson shook his head. "The trouble is that you are right-handed. A right-handed artist ordinarily hatches in the other direction, downward from right to left. Try copying the drawings of Leonardo da Vinci some day; you will have the same difficulty, for Leonardo was also left-handed."

"You mean the government artist, the one who drew these lines on the real money, was left-handed?" Dickory asked.

"Not at all. Remember, this is a printed engraving, not a drawing. Look at your lines in the mirror; that's how they were engraved. When the engraved plates are inked and printed, they appear in reverse on the paper —on the printed bill. Therefore, the government engraver was the one who is right-handed."

"Maybe the counterfeiter didn't know that engravings print in reverse."

"My counterfeiter knew very well that a plate must be engraved in reverse," Noserag said confidently, "otherwise the number 5's would be backward."

Dickory understood. "The counterfeiter is left-handed."

"And the case is solved, Sergeant Kod. Solved!"

"Is that you, Chief?" Inspector Noserag muttered into the telephone. "I got the real dope on the counterfeiter; all it takes is some leg work at your end."

"Who is this?" a baffled Quinn asked. "It sounds like a bad imitation of Humphrey Bogart."

Inspector Noserag cleared his throat and threw down his hat. "It's me, Garson. Just wanted to see if you were on your toes. I thought you might want to hear an artist's humble opinion of the face on the five-dollar bill."

"Go ahead."

"He is an engraver, a professional engraver; so I'd check out the engravers' union, if I were you, and printing plants."

"Thanks a lot, Garson, we've already done that."

"Not with my description, you haven't. Listen carefully, Quinn; show the portrait on the phony bill and say: 'Imagine this man, perhaps older and with a bigger nose.' Check out plastic surgeons, too. He's a flashy dresser; he's left-handed; and he has red thumbs with broken nails. He is a pistachio-nut freak."

"What?"

"Pistachio nuts."

"Good-bye." Quinn hung up abruptly.

"Have you ever encountered a person whose face was out of drawing, Sergeant Kod?" The hats were on again. "Plastic surgery, usually. Sometimes an entire face has been redone, due to an accident or a fire; but mostly it is the result of a simple nose job. Consider, if you will, the nose in my counterfeiter's self-portrait. That short, insignificant blob does not fit into the lines and planes of a face that had molded itself around a former nose of more interesting proportions. There is no doubt in my mind, whatever, that my vain counterfeiter has had his nose bobbed," Inspector Noserag declared.

"Maybe it was just wishful thinking."

"No. My vain engraver fudged the portrait to make himself younger, more handsome; but he was too competent an artist to give himself a nose like that. That blob is the work of a bungling plastic surgeon who gave no thought to the underlying facial structure."

Dickory studied the portrait and agreed, but there was still one clue she couldn't fathom: flashy dresser.

"Rudimentary, my dear Kod. Any man who wears a diamond stickpin in his necktie must be considered ostentatious, to say the least."

"I didn't see any diamond stickpin."

"Neither did I, at first. What appeared to be an error in engraving, or a marred plate, was revealed as a diamond stickpin under my magnifying lens."

"That's not fair," complained Sergeant Kod.

4

For the rest of the week Garson was Garson, and Dock was Dock. And the derelict snoozed and the blind man paced, back and forth, back and forth, just like her brother Donald.

Garson, always present, worked on the Cookie Panzpresser portrait. Dickory cleaned and recleaned the mysteriously messy taboret, and opened the door to parrot-beaked Smith, bat-eared Smith, splay-footed Smith, and chinless Jones. Once the sound of a crying woman was heard from the downstairs apartment; another time, the loud complaints of an angry and defeated man. Each time Garson poured himself another drink.

Dickory stopped to watch Garson paint in his meticulous details. She was worried about him. His black eye had healed, but he would be under Mallomar's fat thumb for the rest of his life. What past crime, she wondered, which one of Quinn's four horsemen was responsible for his being blackmailed—vanity or greed, jealousy or hatred? Vanity seemed the most likely, but surely Garson would have disguised that failing rather than exaggerate it.

The telephone rang. Dickory answered, hoping it would be the chief of detectives with news of the pistachio-nut addict. "Yes, Mrs. Panzpresser . . . Cookie. . . . Yes, the portrait is just about finished." She frowned. "Good-bye!" She slammed the phone angrily.

"What's the matter?" Garson asked. "Did she call you Hickory Dickory Dock?" He was painting a tiny figure in the tiny landscape on the tiny cup in Cookie's long and graceful hand.

"The whole bit," Dickory explained glumly, "with 'the clock struck one, the mouse had fun.' "

"Hickory Dickory Dock." Garson ended the rhyme to Dickory's dismay. "I'm sorry, Dickory, I couldn't help it. You know, Chief Quinn was right about it being a happy name. Besides, a name is just a label; it can stand for whatever a person makes of it." He left off painting to look at his sulking apprentice. "Have you ever heard of Christina Rossetti?"

"No, and that's not a funny name or a happy name." Dickory was screwing and unscrewing the same cap on the same tube of paint.

"I'm talking about names being symbols for who and what you are," Garson said, returning to his canvas. "Christina Rossetti was a poet, a wonderful poet. She was also a bit loony, but that's not the point."

Dickory set down the paint tube and listened.

"Christina Rossetti was a shy, a very shy creature, who

had difficulty speaking to anyone but her family and a few intimate friends. Well, one evening, somehow or other, she found herself at a party. No one noticed her: small, retiring, dressed in black, she sat like a shadow against the wall while the fashionable people flirted, and flaunted their ignorance, and chattered their silly chatter. Then the subject turned to poetry. You can imagine what was said: 'No one has time to read poetry anymore,' or 'All the good poets are dead,' or 'I don't know much about poetry, but I know what I like.' Whatever was said was shallow and stupid, so shallow and stupid that our timid poet stood up and walked to the center of the room. Suddenly all was quiet. All eyes were on this small nervous woman in dull black. Can you guess what she said, Dickory?"

"What?"

"Head held high, she stood tall as she could in the middle of those frightening people and said: 'I am Christina Rossetti.' Then she turned and sat down."

"That's all?"

"That's everything. 'I am Christina Rossetti,' she said, which meant: 'I am a poet, a very good poet.' Those in the room who recognized her name realized they had been speaking rubbish; and those who did not understand were silenced by their ignorance. 'I am Christina Rossetti' was all she need have said. Do you understand what I'm saying, Dickory Dock? Worry less about your name, and more about who you are and who you want to be, and what Dickory Dock will stand for."

Dickory Dock already worried about who she was and what she wanted to be. She worried enough for two Dickory Docks.

"Listen, here is something Christina Rossetti wrote." Garson put down his brush in deference to the poet's words:

"My heart is like a singing bird
   Whose nest is in a watered shoot.
My heart is like an apple-tree
   Whose boughs are bent with thickset fruit."

Dickory's heart had never felt like a singing bird, but it was good poetry, better than the original Isaac Bicker-staffe's. And Garson had told a good story—a story that would nearly cost her her life.

"Has your heart ever felt like a singing bird?" Dickory asked George after they had both signed their names petitioning the mayor for improved street-sign designs.

"Mine will, some day," Harold Silverfish butted in. "When I paint my first masterpiece."

"I doubt that," Professor D'Arches said, folding his petition. "If you are ever that satisfied with your own work, it would be time to give up art and take up plumbing."

George, painfully aware of his lack of sophistication, didn't answer until they were several blocks from school, alone. "My heart once felt like a singing bird, Dickory," he confessed. "It happened a few years ago, back home. I found this bird with a broken wing, a beautiful spotted bird, a thrush. I took it home with me and. . . ."

"George, I don't think that 'my heart is like a singing bird' has anything to do with birds," Dickory said impatiently.

"I know; it just happened that way. I found this bird and. . . . Hi!" George greeted the strange man who blocked their way.

Black hair, black moustache, dark glasses, a gold earring in one ear, and a tattoo on his left arm that was extended toward Dickory. "Deliver this letter for me, young lady. Here's a buck for your pains." His voice was guttural with a trace of an unrecognizable accent.

Two words were scrawled across the sealed envelope in Dickory's hand: *Manny Mallomar*. When she looked up again, the bulky sailor in striped jersey and bell-bottom pants was entering a building, stepping over a derelict asleep in the entranceway.

"Who was that?" George asked.

Dickory's eyes were still on the entranceway. The sign read: HEALTH CLUB AND GYM. And the derelict was the same bum who sprawled on the stoop in Cobble Lane.

"Gee, Dickory, either you've got to cheer up or tell me what's bothering you."

Dickory did neither. "Where should we eat, George? I don't feel much like pizza."

They bought hot dogs and soda from a street vendor and ate on a bench in Washington Square Park. "My park," George called, delighted at having discovered this patch of green. Dickory gave him a patronizing smile. She had known this park from childhood; on hot days her brother had taken her here to romp in the fountain.

"You know," George said after devouring his frank-furter, "I don't even know if Dickory is your first name or your last."

"You have mustard on your chin," she replied. George wiped his chin with a paper napkin and waited for her answer.

"Dickory Dock."

"Hi, Dickory Dock," he said. No snickering, no laughter, no nursery rhyme. There could be only one explanation for this aloof acceptance of her silly name—his name must be sillier. Perhaps he wasn't joking when he said this was his park. "George Washington?" Dickory guessed.

George Washington nodded. "First in war, first in peace, first in the heart of his countrymen. Unless you'd rather discuss the cherry tree."

"I'm the last one to joke about names, George."

He smiled. "It's really George Washington the Third, but no relation to the father of our country. My grandfather, on coming here, wanted to sound like a real American, so he gave the immigration people a name that was more American than his unpronounceable one. He settled in Vermont. That's where I come from, a little town in Vermont; but I'm staying here with an uncle who. . . ."

"I've got to get going," Dickory said abruptly. George looked hurt. "I do want to hear about your family, but I must go. You see, I don't really live in Cobble Lane; I just work there. I live on Fourteenth Street and First." For a moment she considered asking George to deliver the letter for her; then she remembered that Mallomar had seen him gawking at the house. And she remembered the painful nose-tweak. "It's better if you don't walk me to my job; I can't explain, but it's for your own good."

Without asking questions, George agreed. He remained on the bench as Dickory rose to leave.

"One more thing, George. Did your heart really feel like a singing bird that time you caught the thrush?"

George brightened. "Not when I found the thrush, Dickory. When its wing healed. When I watched it fly away. After I nursed it back to health and it flew away free, that's when my heart was like a singing bird."

With the envelope clutched tightly in her hand, Dickory turned the corner into Cobble Lane. From the opposite direction the chief's car slowly turned into the bend, honking its horn to warn the blind man. The derelict, having just settled down on his stoop, opened a bleary eye and closed it again.

"Hickory Dickory Dock,
  The mouse ran up the clock,
    The clock struck four,
    He opened the door,
  Just like Hickory Dickory Dock."

Dickory didn't mind the rhyme today, but not because of the Christina Rossetti story or George's funnier name. "Hello, Chief Quinn," she said loudly and cheerily, grateful to have this official-looking, cigar-smoking bodyguard at her side as she handed the letter through the crack in Mallomar's door.

"Welcome." Garson descended the stairs from the upper floor as Dickory and the chief entered the studio. "Any news on the counterfeiter?" he asked, buttoning the cuffs of his shirt at his wrists.

"Ah, yes, the counterfeiter. Much to the consternation of the feds," the chief announced with pride, "Winston S. Fiddle was apprehended by the New York City Police Department, Bureau of Detectives."

The name sounded familiar to both Garson and Dickory.

"It should sound familiar," Quinn said. "That egomaniac not only put his face on the five-dollar bill, he also signed his name to it. No one bothered to find out who was Secretary of the Treasury when those counterfeit bills were in circulation."

Garson slumped in his chair. Dickory tried to remember who the Secretary of the Treasury was now. She couldn't.

"You were right on all the other details, though," the chief had to admit. "And sooner or later we would have found him, either through the engravers' union or plastic surgeons. Fiddle did have a nose job; and he did eat red pistachio nuts (three pounds a day, in fact); and he was older than he appeared in his portrait; and he was left-handed."

"How did you find him?" Garson asked.

"A bit of dumb luck, dumb meaning Fiddle the engraver. He decided to print ten million dollars more. Ten million bucks takes a lot of paper, you know. Tons of paper. The floor collapsed—paper, printing press, and all. The police emergency crew found Fiddle buried under an avalanche of phony five-dollar bills."

"Dead?" asked Dickory.

"No, just a broken left arm."

"An ironic and just punishment," Garson commented.

"A rather unusual case altogether," Quinn remarked. "Have you noticed that two of the four horsemen of crime were involved here? Vanity *and* Greed. I'm afraid your next case was instigated by greed alone."

"Next case?"

The chief nodded. "I call it The Case of the Full-Sized Midget."

The Case of the
Full-Sized Midget

1

"Fifty-seven witnesses?"

"Actually fifty-six," the chief replied. "One of them is the midget, but we don't know which. Here are the facts:

"The Empress Fatima bracelet was stolen from its display case in the showroom of Opalmeyer Jewelers at 3:15 yesterday afternoon. The glass in one side of the display case was broken, setting off the alarm and automatically locking all exits, including the elevator doors. Fifty-seven people were present when the robbery was committed. They were thoroughly searched, and so was the entire floor. The bracelet was gone."

"Windows?" Garson thought the bracelet could have been thrown out to an accomplice.

"The windows are sealed. Besides, Opalmeyer Jewelers is on the ninety-ninth floor."

"Are you saying that fifty-six people saw a midget steal the bracelet? And that the midget is no longer a midget? And that the bracelet has disappeared even though all doors and windows were locked?"

Quinn shrugged. "Who knows? Everyone panicked when the alarm went off and the guards drew their guns. Here's the complete file on the case." He tossed a thick manila envelope on the table and turned toward the door, listening to the heavy footsteps on the stairs.

The experienced chief of detectives showed neither surprise nor alarm when the mutilated deaf-mute clumped into the studio. Only his cigar moved, from one corner of his mouth to the other. With a hard, professional eye, Quinn watched Isaac Bickerstaffe prop the framed portrait of Mrs. Julius B. Panzpresser against the wall, shuffle over to the mysterious easel, wrap the hidden canvas in its red velvet drape, and carry it from the room.

"Well, I've got to get going," the chief said, rising, but instead of going to the door, he walked to the window. "As if I didn't have enough on my hands these days, what with the stolen Empress Fatima bracelet and an unsolved murder with a missing corpse, the Eldon F. Zyzyskczuk case has just been dropped in my lap."

"I thought Zyzyskczuk wasn't your affair," Garson said. Dickory was still puzzling over the secret canvas Isaac had taken from the studio.

"It wasn't," Quinn replied, brushing ashes from his vest as he looked down on Cobble Lane. "The two Eldon F. Zyzyskczuks was just a matter of mistaken identity and haywire computers. Now it's become criminal fraud to the tune of half a million bucks." He turned to leave. "There are now THREE Eldon F. Zyzyskczuks, heaven help me."

Still baffled, Dickory stared at the empty easel as she capped the tubes of oil paint that cluttered the taboret top.

Garson undressed the dummy drum majorette. "We'll begin on The Case of the Full-Sized Midget tomorrow—it's Saturday, isn't it?—after you return from the Panzpressers."

"What?"

"Julius Panzpresser won't be home, so I thought you would like to deliver the portrait. Cookie will give you a private showing of the collection, if you'd like."

Dickory would like that very much.

"The painting is too heavy for you to manage by yourself," Garson continued, "so Isaac will go with you. Just don't let him out of your sight. He's frightened of the city and could never find his way back home."

How does a brain-damaged monster act when frightened? Dickory decided not to think about it. At least she didn't have to worry about getting mugged in the subway, not with Isaac Bickerstaffe at her side.

"Come over here and tell me what you think of Cookie's portrait," Garson said, setting the ornately framed painting on his easel for display.

Dickory looked at the poised, well-groomed, well-mannered lady pouring tea. "The frame is beautiful."

"And Mrs. Panzpresser?" Garson asked.

"Vain."

"And the painting? What do you think of the painting, Dickory?"

"Slick."

The artist sighed. "You're a hard woman, Dickory Dock. Most uncharitable. What you are looking at is not a portrait of a person, but a portrait of a dream—Cookie Panzpresser's dream."

"It's a vain dream," replied the honest Dickory.

Dickory and Isaac, his face hidden behind the portrait held high, were told to wait in the luxurious entrance of the Panzpresser mansion.

"Hickory Dickory Dock,
The mouse ran up the clock. . . ."

Dickory tugged down the framed painting to reveal Isaac's horrible one-eyed glare. Cookie Panzpresser, rhyming and skipping down the wide, carpeted stairway, stopped dead in her tracks. The toothy grin, which Garson had transformed into a Mona Lisa smile in the portrait, fell into a slack-jawed gape.

"I'm so glad you could come," Mrs. Panzpresser said hesitantly, staring at Isaac. Then she saw the painting. "Is that really me?" she exclaimed with delight. "How wonderful, how absolutely glorious! Julius will just love it, seeing his wife so distinguished and everything."

Watching the exuberant Cookie, Dickory realized Garson had been wrong. Cookie Panzpresser had barely recognized the "lady" in the portrait. It was not *her* dream he had painted, it was the dream of Julius Panzpresser. If so, Dickory did not like Julius. She much preferred Cookie the way she was, a cheerleader, a pink and prancing drum majorette. A drum majorette!

"Oh, but here I am going on and on about my picture when I promised Garson I'd show you the art collection." Linking her arms into theirs, Cookie Panzpresser propelled Dickory and Isaac through a paneled door into a white marble gallery. "I don't know much about these things—it's Julius' collection, you know—now let me see, I think this one here is the Gauguin."

It was a Degas. It was beautiful. It was the tender portrait of a blind woman; a portrait of a real being, who had lived and had loved and knew pain.

Dickory gasped at the vibrant yet tranquil lushness of

the next painting. Gauguin had painted not another's, but his own idyllic dream. Lost in colors, Dickory had forgotten about Isaac Bickerstaffe until she heard his hoarse animal grunts from the other side of the room. Isaac was gesticulating wildly before one of the paintings on the wall, uttering rasping cries and unintelligible moans that in no way resembled sounds of human origin.

Running, skidding across the gallery floor, Cookie and Dickory reached the mad creature at the same time. He had done no damage, but he kept up his howls of joy, or was it despair?

"I think he's trying to say he likes the frame," Dickory shouted above the mute's ravings.

"There, there, young man, everything is going to be all right." Cookie cooed and patted Isaac's arm, comforting him into silence.

Now Dickory studied the unfamiliar painting that had sent Isaac into his spell. "Fruit Peddler" by Edgar Sonneborg (1935–   ), the plaque said. It was a harsh portrait of a rouged woman in tatters straddling a pushcart full of fruit. Head thrown back, she was laughing shamelessly at the hungry hordes that surrounded her cart, saluting them with a peeled banana. The artist's bold, almost frenzied brush had sketched the peddler in brittle colors, in naked and tragic truth; yet the sordidness was somehow fused with compassion. Sonneborg, whoever he was, had painted a portrait of a woman's soul.

Isaac Bickerstaffe was panting heavily from his maniacal exertions, his head weighed down by confusion.

"I think we'd better go now, Mrs. Panzpresser. Thank you for showing me your husband's collection."

"Come back any time, Dickory Dock," Mrs. Panzpresser said warmly. "And thanks so much for bringing the portrait; I can't wait until Julius sees it. Good-bye, Mr. Bickerstaffe, it was so nice meeting you."

2

Inspector Noserag was sorting the photographs of the fifty-seven witnesses when Dickory returned to the studio. "Don your hat, Sergeant Kod, we have no time to lose."

Helmeted, Dickory sat beside him at the library table and suggested they begin with the bracelet. "Length: Ten inches."

"Ten inches long? Incredible," Noserag exclaimed. "The Empress Fatima was corpulent, which of course has nothing to do with this case. Go on."

"Width: Four inches. Consists of six chain-linked identical segments, gold clasp with safety catch."

"Aha! Not pin-linked. The thief would not have had time to take it apart and dispose of the segments separately. The bracelet was stolen in one piece, one piece ten inches long and four inches wide."

"Did you think it might have been taken apart?"

"I think of everything, Sergeant, everything." Inspector Noserag drew deep on his pipe and exhaled a lopsided smoke ring.

Dickory continued. "Each segment consists of one ten-carat diamond surrounded by a rosette of emeralds and. . . ."

"Never mind that part; let's get on to the floor plan."

Head to head (or hat to helmet) they pored over the layout of the ninety-ninth floor. Dickory was getting dizzy from the pipe under her nose.

"Now, Sergeant Kod," Garson said, straightening, "how would you remove yourself from these premises if you were a bracelet ten inches long and four inches wide?"

Having wiped her smarting eyes with the back of her hand, Dickory again studied the floor plan, trying to imagine herself as a bracelet. "The air-conditioning or heating ducts?"

The inspector pointed a shaky finger at a notation on the plan. "The ducts are in the ceiling, which is twelve feet high. Anyone climbing to that height, especially a midget, would surely have been noticed, even in a panic. But there is another way out for an object that size. Look in the hall next to the elevators."

"The mail slot?"

"Indeed! My thief carried a padded, stamped, and addressed envelope in his pocket. He slipped the bracelet into the envelope, sealed it—or perhaps it was self-sealing —and, unnoticed in the ensuing panic, deposited it into the mail slot. A daring feat, brilliantly planned and executed. When was the crime committed, at what time?"

"Three-fifteen in the afternoon."

"Make a note, Sergeant. I, Inspector Noserag, surmise that the Empress Fatima bracelet was placed in an envelope, dropped into the mail chute, and collected by the postman from the ground-floor box no later than three-thirty."

"Very good, Inspector," Dickory remarked. "Now, all we have to do is find out who mailed the bracelet, and to whom."

"Precisely."

In their photographs the fifty-seven witnesses stood tall and short (but not short enough), in attitudes ranging from self-conscious to indignant. Some slouched, some leaned, and one thumbed his nose at the camera.

"Hmmmmm," murmured the inspector.

The identity of the jewel thief was still a deep mystery, but the character of Inspector Noserag had finally emerged. His voice was deliberate, upper-class yet tough. His shoulders were slumped, his back bowed from a lifetime spent tracking footprints. All that remained of Garson was a tremor in his right hand.

Kod was still Dickory wearing a funny hat.

Pipe-puffing Inspector Noserag, shoulders slumped, hands clasped behind his bowed back, moved in his typical long-legged, bent-kneed stride down the length of the table and back, studying the faces in the long row of photographs. He was followed by Sergeant Kod.

"Bah, photographs prevaricate," he grumbled. "Cameras lie. These are pictures of masks worn consciously or unconsciously by the posers. Red hair appears black; eyes are in shadow; the curve of the chin, the contour of the cheek are flattened onto the two-dimensional emulsified paper as though the faces had been rolled under a paving machine."

Still studying the photographs, Dickory thought these likenesses came closer to the truth than Garson's dream portraits did.

The inspector sighed wearily. "Nevertheless, these hazy imitations of fifty-seven living and breathing mortals are all we have to go on, for the nonce." Dickory bumped into Noserag when he suddenly stopped. "Now, Sergeant Kod, before we study the testimony and before we become entangled in facts, do you have any intuitive choice?"

"Yes, I do," Dickory replied, setting her helmet straight. "The crime took a lot of nerve. It was pulled off right in the middle of the day in front of fifty-six witnesses. Our man was not a sneak thief."

"Good thinking, Sergeant. And your audacious culprit is whom?"

"The man thumbing his nose."

Inspector Noserag reached across the table for the nose-thumber's photograph (average size, average build, glasses, wearing a suit and necktie) and turned to the information taped to the back.

TIMOTHY HAY
    Date of birth: 3/15/38. Sex: M.
    Height: 5–10. Eyes: Hazel.
    Corrective lenses.
    Occupation: Underwear salesman.
Reason for being on premises:
    Bought pearls for wife's birthday.
Location at time of robbery:
    At pearl counter.
Testimony:
    Says he seen nothing. Says he will
    sue N.Y.C. for money lost in missing
    3:30 appt. with important buyer (confirmed).
Attitude of witness:
    Uncooperative.

"Timothy Hay sounds like a fake name," Dickory said.

"The stranger the name, the more likely it's real," Noserag instructed. "No, Timothy Hay is definitely his real name. Not only was his appointment confirmed, but compare the phrase 'corrective lenses' with 'says he seen nothing.' The illiterate who wrote this report copied the vital statistics from a driver's license."

"Have you considered that a 3:30 appointment is an excellent alibi, Inspector?"

"Naturally," Noserag replied huffily. "Everything is possible, and anyone could be the thief. Except Timothy Hay."

"And why not Timothy Hay?"

"Deductive introspection, Kod. What better pose of innocence than to place the guilt on someone else. My clever thief would have been very quick to point his finger at someone else, or at least confuse the police with a misleading description." Inspector Noserag had developed a habit of using the personal possessive when referring to the criminal. "My clever thief," he had said. Perhaps he was trying to place himself in the mind of the offender, Dickory thought, or perhaps there was some of the larcenist in Garson's own soul.

"Not only can we eliminate Timothy Hay," Noserag continued, "we can eliminate those witnesses who testified to seeing nothing."

Each took a stack of photographs and sorted through the testimony on the reverse sides. "Says he seen nothing" occurred nineteen more times. Dickory added them to the reject pile along with Timothy Hay (the haystack, she called it).

"Twenty witnesses rejected," the inspector remarked. "Which, if I am not mistaken, leaves us with only thirty-eight suspects."

"Thirty-seven," said Sergeant Kod.

Thirty-seven witnesses had described the thief. From their testimony, Noserag and Kod compiled a report indicating the number of times each feature was mentioned:

Male (20).   Female (17).
Height: Midget (4).   Short (10).   Average (23).
Weight: Thin to average (35).   Fat (2).
Hair: Red (4).   Blond (7).   Brown (18).   Black (8).
Eyes: Blue (6).   Brown (8).   Did not notice (23).
Clothes: Blue suit (5).   Brown suit (3).   Gray suit (1).
   Black dress (1).   Print dress (1).   Blue zippered
   jacket, no tie (22).   Did not notice (4).
Distinguishing marks: Harelip (4).   None (33).

"What do you make of this confusion, Sergeant?"

"I think everybody's lying, or else everybody did it," Dickory replied.

Noserag blew another irregular smoke ring into the smoke-filled air. "This reminds me of a devilishly difficult case I solved several years ago . . . never mind." Unable to invent a story fast enough, he rose and strode to the front window. "Sergeant Kod, you are an observant person. In fact, my dear friend Garson has testified to your keen awareness and descriptive ability."

Perhaps it was due to her poor acting ability, but Noserag was confusing Dock with Kod.

"Sergeant, have you been aware of a snaggle-toothed blind man walking his German shepherd up and down this street?"

"Yes."

"Quickly now, tell me in which ear he wears a gold earring."

"The left?"

"No guessing. You are an eyewitness. Is it or is it not the left ear?"

"Yes." Dickory had been forced to commit herself. "The gold earring is in the left ear."

"Wrong!" The inspector spun around and stared at Dickory. "You are totally and unequivocally wrong, Sergeant Kod. In the first instance, the snaggle-toothed blind man has straight, even teeth—a fact which you did not bother to correct. In the second instance, the blind man's earring is not gold; in fact, he is wearing no earring at all. And in the third instance. . . ."

Resenting his ridicule, Dickory turned her back on him and walked into the studio. Garson followed and placed his hand on her shoulder. "Come, Dickory, don't take it so hard. I was just trying to prove a point. If an astute observer like you can be badgered into giving false testimony, you can imagine how thirty-seven simple-eyed, panicky witnesses could get so mixed up. Come, let's begin again."

Once again Dickory studied the composite descriptions. "Twenty-two witnesses saw a man in a blue zippered jacket, no tie. There's a photo of him somewhere."

"Class snobbery, that's all. Probably a messenger. The rich think only the poor are thieves. Hah!"

Dickory tried again. "The number *4* appears more often than any other number. Four people seem to be agreeing on something."

"Excellent, Sergeant Kod, excellent. And what exactly do the four witnesses agree on?"

"Midget. Red hair. Did not notice clothes. Harelip."

"Quick, Sergeant, to the easel." Noserag dashed to the police easel, stared at the blank canvas, unbuttoned his cuff, then, deciding not to roll up his sleeves, buttoned it again.

Still seated, Dickory was sorting through the photographs knowing that Garson would soon return.

"Did you say a red-headed midget with a harelip?" he asked, walking slowly back to the library table.

"Yes. And not one of the fifty-seven witnesses is a redhead or a midget or has a harelip." Sergeant Kod handed him the pictures of the four people who had supplied that testimony.

"Indeed," Noserag exclaimed. "It is just as I surmised. My clever thief provided a false description that was testified to by three gullible bystanders. There was no red-headed midget with a harelip. One of these four witnesses is my real thief."

Dickory could not understand how three people could agree on having seen a midget who wasn't there.

"Not at all surprising," Noserag explained. "What surprises me more is that there were only three such gullible witnesses. Imagine the scene, Sergeant, alarms blaring, guards with drawn guns. Some people ducked or fell to their knees; and in the panic, three witnesses saw midgets. Some people bit their lips in fear; and three witnesses saw harelips."

Eyes closed, Dickory pictured the scene, but she saw no redhead in it.

"The red hair is what I call memory displacement," Noserag said with authority. "Earlier in the day three witnesses had glimpsed a person with flaming red hair. Upon hearing the false description, they displaced that memory to the ninety-ninth floor."

Now Dickory remembered. The gold earring had been in the ear of the tattooed sailor who had given her the letter for Manny Mallomar.

Three gullible witnesses and one thief. The photographs of the four people who had described the red-headed midget with a harelip lay face up on the table: a squinting old man in uniform; a thin, nervous woman in a print dress; an elderly businessman; and an idiot-faced young delivery boy. One by one Dickory read the testimony aloud to the slouched and smoking inspector.

"ANGUS STUMPF, elevator operator.
Reason for being on premises: works there.
Location at time of robbery: in elevator.
Testimony: My elevator had just opened at the ninety-ninth floor and the passengers were filing out into the showroom, when *bam!* the alarm goes off. That shuts off power to the elevator, can't even shut the doors if it's open like mine was. So everybody starts running in all directions, mostly into each other, and yelling. I come out of my elevator to get a good look, my eyes not being what they used to be, but that's all right, driving an elevator's not like driving a truck, you know. Then I sees him: a red-headed midget with a harelip. He's the one all right, all right.
Attitude of witness: Talkative.

"That leaves him out," Dickory continued. "Angus Stumpf couldn't have been riding up in the elevator and stealing the bracelet at the same time. But he was standing next to the mail slot—maybe he's an accomplice."

"I doubt that, Sergeant. It would be too dangerous a caper for more than one person. No, I'm quite certain my clever thief did it alone. Next?"

"HORTENSE FREEMARTIN, bookkeeper at the S & S Sausage Company.
Reason for being on premises: to look at the Empress Fatima bracelet.
Location at time of robbery: looking at the Empress Fatima bracelet.

Testimony: I was looking at the Empress Fatima bracelet. I glanced up when the President of the United States came in. Then the alarm went off, right next to me. I nearly had a heart attack I was so scared. The next thing I saw was a midget run by. I'm sure I saw him, red hair, harelip, and all.

Attitude of witness: Nervous.

"The President of the United States?" Dickory reached for the haystack of rejected photographs.

"Obviously a diversionary tactic by my thief to draw attention away from the glass display case. Go on, Sergeant."

"This is the young guy in the zippered jacket and no tie.

"JOACHIM NESSELRODE, delivery boy for the Quickee Coffee Shoppee.

Reason for being on premises: delivering six cofees—five regular, one black; and four Danishes—three cheese, one prune.

Location at time of robbery: can't remember.

Testimony: First I see the President of the United States. Then I hear a loud alarm, like a fire, I think. Then I look for a midget with red hair and a hairy lip. Then I see him, then I don't.

Attitude of witness: Cooperative.

Possibly mentally deficient.

"What a perfect disguise," Dickory added.

"Too perfect." Noserag waved at her to continue.

"F. (Frederick) K. (Kurt) OPALMEYER, owner of Opalmeyer Jewelers.

Reason for being on premises: owns the place.

Location at time of robbery: checking on the Empress Fatima bracelet.

Testimony: I went to the display case to check on the bracelet. It was still there when someone shouted, "Good afternoon, Mr. President." I looked up, since I'm the president of Opalmeyer Jewelers. Suddenly, I heard glass breaking and the alarm went off. I looked down at the case; the bracelet was gone. Gone, oh me, oh my! (blows nose, wipes eyes). Excuse me. Then I thought I saw the thief dodging through the crowd. I ran after him, but he disappeared. Red hair. Harelip. A midget, he must have been a midget, else how could he steal the bracelet without being seen? The bracelet, the beautiful bracelet. It was my dumb brother-in-law's idea to borrow it in the first place. Free publicity, he said. Some publicity, I could do without such publicity. A two-million-dollar bracelet, stolen in my own shop, under my very nose. Why did it have to happen to me. What have I done to deserve such a fate?

Attitude of witness: Depressed.

Note: brother-in-law in Europe on business.

"I still think the delivery boy did it," Dickory said. "And I live in a tenement, so it's not class snobbery."

Inspector Noserag accepted the fact that a police sergeant could live in a tenement. He puffed and puffed and hmmmed and hmmmed. Suddenly he sprung from his chair. "I must call Quinn immediately."

Dickory grabbed the deerstalker hat from his head just in time. "Hello, Chief? Garson here. I've got your man. I know who stole the Empress Fatima bracelet."

"Who?"

"Hang on to your chair, Chief. It was F. K. Opalmeyer."

"Really?"

"And he mailed the bracelet to himself, probably to his home address. If I were you, I'd get a search warrant before Opalmeyer skips town."

"I'll do that. Thanks, Garson. And if you're right, I'm coming over to congratulate you and find out how you did it. Maybe I can learn something."

"See you soon, then," Garson replied confidently.

Quinn chuckled as he hung up the telephone. "He says it's Opalmeyer," he reported to his assistant. "A clever man, our Garson. I'll be going over there in an hour; see that my little surprise is ready."

Chief Quinn had solved The Case of the Full-Sized Midget two days ago. F. K. Opalmeyer was already behind bars.

3

Savoring his moment of triumph, Garson himself opened the front door. "Welcome, Chief Quinn. I assume you have apprehended the perpetrator."

"One half hour after you called," Quinn lied with a big smile. "Congratulations, Garson. Or is it Sherlock Holmes? And Doctor Watson, I presume."

"Hello, Chief," Dickory said, looking around to see if the hats had been left out. They were out of sight; the chief was joking.

Garson sat down in the wing chair with a drink, but Quinn refused to join him. Casually, he toured the studio. "Out of work, I see," he remarked, glancing at the empty easels. "And what's this?" He stopped before one of the naked manikins. "I could have you arrested for indecent exposure, Madam, or is it Sir?" The chief certainly was in good humor.

"I gather you not only captured the jewel thief, but recovered the bracelet as well," Garson guessed.

"Thanks to you, we certainly did." The chief walked into the kitchen area. "Don't bother, Hickory, I can pour my own coffee. I've been here too often to be treated as a guest." At last the chief sat down. "Now, tell me how you did it."

"Professional secret," Garson replied coolly. "But I can tell you how Opalmeyer did it. You see, there would not have been time to break the glass, then steal the bracelet *after* the alarm went off. Opalmeyer had a key. When someone—probably Opalmeyer himself—shouted about the President, he unlocked the case, took out the bracelet, and locked the case again. When he smashed the glass, the bracelet was already in the envelope in his pocket."

"Well, what do you know," said the chief.

"Very clever of Opalmeyer," Garson continued. "If he had been caught taking the bracelet, he would have been innocent of any crime. He was, after all, president of the company. But no one saw him. In the pretense of running after a thief, Opalmeyer dashed into the hallway, dropped the envelope into the mail slot, then gave his loud description of the nonexistent midget."

"What was the motive, Chief?" Dickory asked. "Greed?"

"No, he wasn't going to sell it, he says," Quinn replied. "Something came over him and he just had to have it. It was the most beautiful thing he'd ever seen, and he wanted to look at it for the rest of his life. Covetousness, I'd call it."

"That's a fifth horseman," Dickory said.

"So it is. All right, change it to greed. Or maybe jealousy. Never in his life's career had he been able to design a masterpiece like that bracelet. Tell me, Garson, you're an artist, a creator. Is jealousy reason enough to make a man steal? Or kill?"

"Kill?" Garson was surprised by the question.

The phone rang. "That's probably for me," the chief said, rising.

Dickory answered. It was Cookie Panzpresser in tears. Her husband didn't like the portrait at all. In fact, he hated it and wanted it out of the house this instant. Oh dear, what was she going to do?

"I'm so sorry, Mrs. Panzpresser, but Garson isn't here right now. I'll give him the message; I'm sure he can work something out. And Mrs. Panzpresser, Cookie, thanks again for letting me see the art collection." Dickory hung up the phone, stamped her foot, glanced at Garson, jumped and stamped again. She smiled sheepishly at his curious look.

"Could have sworn that phone call was for me," Quinn said, strangely unaware of Dickory's stomping. "The Zyzyskczuk case has got the whole department at wit's end."

"Maybe I can help," Garson offered.

"Yes, maybe you can. The trouble is that the two Eldon F. Zyzyskczuks refuse to meet or even speak to each other," Quinn explained, having resumed his chair. "And we still have no idea where to find number three."

"That's understandable," Garson said. "Anyone who grew up with a name like Eldon F. Zyzyskczuk, thinking himself unique, can't admit that there could be another person with the same name. Except when it comes to a wrong bill." Suddenly he jumped, crunched his heel on the floor in front of him, then leaned back in his chair as if nothing had happened.

Again the chief did not seem to notice. "Here's what we have: Eldon F. Zyzyskczuk, the importer, is medium-sized everything: sandy hair, brown eyes, rimless glasses, a bachelor. He has a neat, slanted handwriting."

"Right-handed?" Garson asked.

"All three are right-handed," Quinn replied. "Now, Eldon F. Zyzyskczuk, the exporter, is a bit shorter, has dark hair and a moustache, blue eyes, a widower with one grown daughter who lives in California, and a nephew who helps in his business. He has a stiff up-and-down handwriting."

Dickory stamped her foot in the kitchen area.

Quinn continued. "Six months ago, the third Eldon F. Zyzyskczuk appeared. There was such a mix-up about the first two, the third went unnoticed until he had bought and sold half the city of New York: real estate, cars, off-track betting schemes, stocks and bonds, you name it."

"Forgery?" Garson asked, staring at the floor.

"That's right. We think it was some sort of inside job; someone knew about the confusion caused by the two names and took advantage of it. That's whose portrait I want you to paint, Garson, the third man, the impostor who forges the names of Eldon F. Zyzyskczuk. I'll send along some of the descriptions, and the witnesses themselves, if you like. He's about five-feet ten, heavy-set, wears sunglasses and gloves."

"Whose signature does he forge, the importer's or the exporter's?"

"Both. Not perfectly, but good enough."

"Nothing else unusual?" Garson ground his foot on the floor.

"Just one thing. He writes holding the pen between his third and fourth fingers. He may have an injured index finger."

This time the telephone call was for the chief. "Sorry, I've got to go." The chief scrambled down the stairs without a good-bye, without even a nursery rhyme.

Dickory stamped her foot again. "Cockroaches," she said. "We're overrun with cockroaches."

"I know," Garson replied with disgust. "I found a few myself. Remind me to call the exterminator tomorrow. What time is it?"

"Exactly five-thirteen."

Garson leaped from his chair and bounded down the stairs.

"Wait, Garson, what should I tell Cookie Panz-presser?"

"Tell her to donate the portrait to the Museum of Modern Art," he said, and slammed the front door.

Dickory remained on the top landing, trying to decide if Garson had been joking. If it was a joke, it was a bad one. Suddenly she realized that she was staring down into the ugly face of Manny Mallomar. She darted into the studio, closing the door behind her, and ran to the window to see if Garson, her protector, was still there.

Garson had just turned beyond the bend. The derelict staggered to his feet and stumbled after him. Dickory's eyes followed the derelict down the street. The upstairs wardrobe contained a costume similar to his, lumberjack shirt and baggy pants, although not quite as disreputable. He looked and staggered and smelled like a real bum, unlike Garson's unsuccessful imitation, but perhaps this man was just a better actor.

The derelict lurched out of sight. Now, in the middle of the street, stood a fat greasy ghost and his skinny black shadow. Shrimps Marinara was pointing her out to the pop-eyed Manny Mallomar. Dickory edged away from the window. When she again looked down, the two ugly tenants disappeared around the bend, and, tapping his cane, so did the blind man. The blind man with the straight teeth and no gold earring in either ear.

4

"The gold earring was in his right ear," George said. He had found a Dock on Fourteenth Street in the telephone book and called Dickory to report having seen the tattooed sailor again. "And you know who he was having dinner with? Guess."

"Who's Guest?" The television set was blaring, but Dickory didn't dare ask her brother to make another trip back and forth to lower the sound.

"I said guess, not guest. Anyhow, it was the cook."

"Who?"

"The sailor was in the café with the cook—the fat man in the white suit, who I saw in the window where you work. I listened to what they said, too. I thought you might want to know about it, because you looked so scared when the sailor handed you the letter."

"Listen, George, I can't hear you very well. Why don't you come over here and tell me about it?"

"I can't. My uncle is out, and I have to stay here and answer his phone." George did not explain how he could answer the telephone when he was talking on it. "How about going to the zoo with me tomorrow to sketch?"

After another "who" and "zoo," it was agreed.

Dickory returned to her assignment wondering why George was so excited about having seen the tattooed sailor with Mallomar. The note had probably set the time and place for that meeting. The sailor did not want to be seen on Cobble Lane, what with Chief Quinn popping in and out.

In a very short time she had finished her design, a composition based on two complementary colors which, in the right proportions, would form gray. She painted a red swash between two fine black lines, then a blue-green swash between the next. The three hatched pen strokes were already on the canvas from The Case of the Face on the Five-Dollar Bill.

At the zoo, George again insisted that the sailor's gold earring had been in his right earlobe. And the tattoo was on his left arm. "It said 'Potato,' " George reported.

"Potato?" Dickory could hardly believe that anyone would want the word "Potato" tattooed on his arm. "Mother," yes, or a sweetheart's name. But "Potato"?

"And it was upside down," George continued. "I had to lean way over to read it."

"An upside-down tattoo that said 'Potato'?" Dickory listened with some skepticism to her friend's account of the meeting between Mallomar and the sailor.

George had followed the sailor into the café and sat

down at the next table with his back toward him. "I was afraid the fat man would recognize me, but he was too upset to notice anything. Except the tattoo. He kept looking at the tattoo, trying to read what it said."

"Why was he upset?" Dickory asked.

"The sailor wanted some sort of list from the fat man. He called him—what was it—Oreo, I think."

"Mallomar."

"That's right, Mallomar. 'Mallomar,' the sailor said, 'you're nothing but a cheap crook. The big boss don't like your busting in on his territory. He wants the list, now; and he wants you to move out of there and leave your files,' or something like that." George blushed at his clumsy imitation of the sailor's speech. "The fat man swore a lot, and the sailor threatened him. Sounded like blackmail to me."

"Who was blackmailing whom?"

"I think the sailor was blackmailing the fat man. Something about a murder in a clock shop. Anyhow, the fat man said that the list was in a safe deposit box and he couldn't get to the bank until Monday. He sure sounded scared. The sailor said, 'Okay, Monday, but don't try anything funny because you're being watched every minute. There's a contract out on you if you don't deliver.'"

George had been seeing too many movies, Dickory thought. It was all so confusing; and if true, made little difference whether Garson was being blackmailed by a little crook or a big one.

"Did you hear the sailor's name?" she asked.

"Yes—no. Yes, I heard the name, but I forgot it. Something that begins with a flower."

"Zinnia?" Dickory guessed, thinking that was close enough to Zyzyskczuk. She wanted to solve the next case all by herself.

"No, not Zinnia. I think it begins with an *R*." That

was the best George could do. He was doing even worse with his sketch of the pacing tiger. "I wish he'd hold still for two minutes," he complained.

"Over here," Dickory said. "The lions are asleep."

"Asleep!" shouted the drawing instructor on viewing the displayed sketches. "Two drawings of sleeping lions, six drawings of people asleep on the subway, one infant asleep in a crib! This is supposed to be life drawing, not dead drawing. These were supposed to have been quick sketches, notes on movement." Fists on his hips, he glowered at the class. "Choke-ups, that's what you are. Afraid one line might be out of place. Maybe it's my own fault for allowing the model to assume five-minute poses. Tomorrow she is going to move. Move, move, move. And you are going to sketch, sketch, sketch."

Eyes downcast, shoulders slumped, Dickory scuffed along the Greenwich Village streets. The ridicule of the life-drawing teacher had been bad enough, but Professor D'Arches had harshly criticized her three-stroke complementary-color design. "A traffic light," he had called it, and went on to rant about his pet peeve, the incompetence and clutter of street signs.

"I'm not much of an artist," she confessed to George, who was shambling at her side.

"Cheer up, Dickory. If you did everything right you wouldn't have to go to art school. The teachers pick on you because you're good. They don't want you to get lazy. Besides, artists have to get used to criticism, lots of it, so better now than later. I'd be happy just to have one of the teachers notice me, no matter what he said."

With that sound advice and a sad wave, George left Dickory at the corner of Cobble Lane. He did not return to school to sketch, sketch, sketch.

Neither did Dickory.

The Case of the
Disguised Disguise

1

Cobble Lane was deserted when Dickory arrived. There was a deathly quiet in and around Number 12. Mallomar's door was closed. She listened. There was no sound within. Garson's door was open. She called. No one answered.

Suddenly an insistent doorbell shattered the silence. A stranger in a nylon jacket, carrying a square, battered case, pushed his way into the house. "Exterminator," he announced. "From the way it sounds, I got to do the whole place. Lead the way—I'll start from the top down."

Dickory led the exterminator up the two flights to the top floor. He filled his can in the bathtub, pumped it, and began to spray. "You don't have to stay; I'll let you know when I'm done. The fumes are bad for you, you know."

Dickory stayed. One of her qualifications for this job was being a born-and-bred New Yorker, and New Yorkers don't trust anyone, not even exterminators. "You should come over to where I live. The exterminator our landlord sends around gives a squirt here and a squirt there, and is in and out in two minutes."

This exterminator opened every closet, pulled out every drawer. He sprayed in every corner of every room. He sprayed so much he had to refill his tank five times before he came down to the studio floor.

There, too, not a cabinet or a shelf was left untouched. He removed drawers, lifted rugs; he even took the telephone apart and sprayed. And sprayed.

"How do I get in downstairs?" he asked.

"Follow me." Dickory had to try several keys on her ring before the door to Mallomar's apartment would open.

The elegant rooms she had seen on the first day of her job were barely recognizable now. Newspapers and empty bottles were strewn over the Oriental rugs; dirty glasses lined the fireplace. The only clean things in the bedroom, where the exterminator was now spraying, were the white suits hanging in the closet. He sprayed the white suits, the white shoes, and the pile of dirty white shirts; he even opened an empty suitcase and sprayed into the inside pockets.

"You're making me nervous," he complained to Dickory. "Don't you have anything else to do?"

"No," she replied, and followed him down the short, curved steps into the living room.

The exterminator opened a file-cabinet drawer.

"You can't spray in there." Dickory slammed the

drawer on his nozzle. Papers incriminating Garson might be in there. Perhaps, after the exterminator left, she would return and. . . .

"I gotta spray in there," the exterminator insisted, opening the drawer again. "I just saw a roach crawl out."

Once more Dickory slammed it shut. The exterminator tried another file drawer; it was locked.

"I can't guarantee this job," he complained.

Dickory led the grumbling exterminator under the balcony into the kitchen, where he sprayed halfheartedly, into the furnace room, which he sprayed even less.

"Here's where the roaches are coming from." He stood before the padlocked storeroom door.

"I don't know the combination," Dickory said. "Why don't you ask the man in there if he knows it?" She pointed to the guest room.

The exterminator knocked on the guest-room door and walked in without waiting for an answer, followed by the curious Dickory.

Blue-checked curtains hung on the windows of the neat and spacious room, matching the spread on the brass bed. There was evidence of woodworking on the workbench, but not a shaving was to be found on the blue rug, not a trace of sawdust hung in the air. Isaac Bickerstaffe, seated in an overstuffed chair, was staring at a large framed painting on the wall.

"Hey, buddy, can you open the padlock?" The exterminator poked the immobile deaf-mute on the arm. "Hey buddy —Awww!" Isaac's awful one-eyed glare sent the intruder dashing out of the room.

Grunting, Isaac turned his one eye on Dickory; his jerking hands pointed to himself and to the portrait. It was a slick Garson painting of a handsome, carefree young man. A large and muscular young man, as he had looked before the accident that had transformed him into Isaac Bickerstaffe.

Isaac's "ung-ung-ung" echoed through the basement as Dickory hurried after the exterminator. He was waiting in the front hallway, his equipment packed, trying to look composed.

"I'm afraid I can't pay you now," she said, opening the front door.

"You don't have to," he said, hurrying out of the house with his black case. "It's all part of the contract."

Manny Mallomar and Shrimps Marinara were standing on the stoop.

2

"Hey, boss," Shrimps shouted, darting behind Dickory. "The door to our rooms is open!"

Counting on the fact that Shrimps hated to be touched, Dickory slowly backed down the hall, step by step, staring into the bulging eyes of her white-suited enemy. Step by step, Mallomar wobbled toward her, his fat hands outstretched like a clumsy child trying to catch a ground-feeding bird. "What's that about a contract, huh, punk?"

Unexpectedly the riser of the bottom step creased Dickory's calf. Her knee buckled. Mallomar lunged. One hand grabbed her neck, the other clasped her wrists behind her back. Struggling, stumbling, she was dragged into the apartment and down the curved stairs by the iron-fisted fat man.

"Get the rope, Shrimps," he snarled as he forced Dickory into a straight chair. Dickory gave up her struggle, for each movement tightened the fat, manicured hand around her throat, pressing her chin upward until she thought her teeth would shatter.

"What were you doing in my apartment?" He leaned over her, growling his question into her face.

She tried to turn her head away from the foul breath. "The exterminator came and. . . ." Mallomar jerked her head up and back. Her teeth tore into her lip. She tasted blood.

"Who's paying you to spy on me?"

"She works for the organization, boss, I keep telling you," Shrimps muttered. "And she's in with the cops."

Dickory tried to move her head to indicate "no."

"What's your name, punk?" Mallomar loosened his grip slightly to allow her to speak.

If the sound of her name really made people happy, now was the time. "Dickory Dock," she croaked hoarsely.

Mallomar tightened his grip on her throat and her wrists.

"She's lying, boss. The cop calls her Hickory. It's a joke, like the nursery rhyme, you know:

"Hickory Dickory Dock,
The mouse ran up the clock,
The clock struck one,
The mouse ran—no, run. . . .

"How does that go?"

"Shut up, you idiot," Mallomar barked. His fingernails dug into the side of Dickory's neck. Blood from her split lip dribbled down her chin. Before her, Shrimps was winding a knotted cord around his hands, a garroting cord that, with one snap against her windpipe, would kill her instantly.

"Let's get this over with, fast," Shrimps urged, walking behind her chair.

Upstairs, the telephone was ringing.

"One last time, you snooping brat," Mallomar snarled. "Shrimps is getting impatient. Now, what did you say your name was?"

"I am Christina Rossetti."

The cord whipped down before her eyes. Hard knots against her throat. A hollow cracking. Telephone ringing. Tin cans falling and bells chiming.

> "Oranges and lemons,"
> say the bells of St. Clements;

The cord fell slack into Dickory's lap.

> "You owe me five farthings,"
> say the bells of St. Martins;

Afraid to look behind her, around her, Dickory ran to the door to the garden at the far end of the room.

> "When will you pay me?"
> say the bells of Old Bailey;

Hands trembling, fumbling with the rusted bolt, she at last jiggled it open and ran into what she thought would be the garden. She was trapped. Dickory shook the iron bars of the tall fence that enclosed the small triangular patch of concrete. Trapped.

> "When I grow rich,"
> say the bells of Shoreditch.

Sobbing with fear, Dickory ran back through the room, to the stairs, into the arms of. . . . She stared down at the colors: chrome yellow, chrome green, cadmium red, cobalt blue. "Potato," she read aloud.

At her feet lay the lifeless bodies of Manny Mallomar and Shrimps Marinara. Mallomar's white suit was splotched with crimson; his popped eyes stared at the high ceiling.

"Get out of here, hurry!" The tattooed sailor shoved her toward the door.

Dickory stumbled on a curved step, scrambled to her feet, and ran out of the house. "Police!" she screamed, clutching the cast-iron newel. "Somebody get the police."

Someone came running. "I'm the police, what's going on in there?" It was the blind man.

"Murder," Dickory whispered, sinking down on the concrete stoop, holding her bruised throat.

Pulling a two-way radio from his pocket, the unblind detective called in his report. "Are you all right?" he asked Dickory, eyes on the front door.

She nodded. She was not all right, but there was nothing anyone could do about it. Numb and hurting, she patted the German shepherd as the street detective, his gun drawn, stood guard at the entrance to number 12.

3

Screaming sirens wavered and died as four patrol cars
screeched into narrow Cobble Lane. Car doors slammed,
radios crackled; heads popped out of the muntined windows of the historic houses as the sharp commands of
police sergeants echoed through the gathering crowd and
bounced off the brick walls.

"Are you all right, Hickory?" Chief Quinn asked.

Still slumped on the stoop, Dickory raised her head
on hearing the familiar voice and nodded unconvinc-
ingly. The derelict-disguised detective nearly tripped
over her as he trotted down the steps. "Nothing upstairs,
Chief. I'll go check out the back."

"Do that, Dinkel," Quinn said. He cupped his hand

under Dickory's chin and placed a finger on her bloodied lip. He raised her head and inspected the raw bruises on her throat. "The wounds aren't serious, but they sure must hurt. Come, let's go inside. Where's Garson?"

"I don't know," she replied weakly, staring at the curiosity-seekers who were pressing and swelling against the restraining arms of the uniformed police. The crowd looked exactly like the morbid mob that had stared through the windows of the pawn shop the night her parents were murdered. Rising, she turned her back on them and followed Chief Quinn into the house.

"Now, go wash your face and comb your hair," he said, treating his dazed eyewitness as he would a small child. "Then I want you to tell me everything that happened here. All right, Hickory?"

"Dickory," she corrected him.

"Dock," he replied to humor her.

> "Hickory Dickory Dock,
>   The mouse ran up the clock,
>   The clock struck five,
>   He's still alive,
>   Just like Hickory Dickory Dock."

Washed and combed, standing on the balcony overlooking the downstairs living room, Dickory once again ached with the remembered fear and pain. She clutched the railing to steady herself.

Cameras flashed. Photographers circled the black and white and crimson bodies like jackals around carrion. Then the detectives swooped down, like buzzards at a feast, and picked the bodies clean. A hand brought up a key ring, and a familiar-looking detective, the exterminator, hurried to the locked file drawer. Another hand passed a wallet to the blind man, who brought it to

Quinn. The exterminator, the blind man, the derelict—
all detectives. A lot of good they were, Dickory thought;
she had almost been killed, right under their big noses.

"What's going on here?" Garson bellowed, barging
through the police barricade. "Where's Dickory?" He
hurried to her side. "What happened? Are you all right?"

Dickory pointed down to the ugly scene. She did feel
better now that Garson was here.

The detectives had moved away from the two bodies
to search the room. A long, black overcoat lay open, ex-
posing a mass of wires, tape recorders, and miniature mi-
crophones strung over Shrimps' skinny frame. Mallomar
looked as repugnant in death as he had in life.

"The ugly dumpling and his mechanical man," Garson said lightly. "Dead, I presume."

Dickory did not respond. She was staring down at
Mallomar's corpse. From a gold chain across his bulging
white vest dangled an open enamel watchcase painted
with roses. Its chimes had unwound into silence.

Quinn ushered his trembling witness up to the studio
floor, where Dickory related her terrifying tale. She described the scene as accurately as she could without men-
tioning blackmail, protecting Garson every step of the
way. Garson sat with his head in his hands, uttering an
occasional self-chastising moan. The chief listened at-
tentively, his face impassive, his cigar still, even when
Dickory told of Shrimps reciting the nursery rhyme.

"They wouldn't believe my name, so I said, 'I am
Christina Rossetti.' "

Garson groaned and reproached himself for having
put her in danger, for having left her alone in the house
while he had gone to his health club for a workout.

"Do you have any idea why Mallomar or Shrimps
wanted to kill you?" Quinn asked.

Dickory shook her head and slowly rose to answer the ringing telephone.

"I'll get it," the chief said firmly. "Hello? Sorry, she can't come to the phone. This is Chief of Detectives Joseph P. Quinn. Yes, I'll take the message. . . . What? Who is this? . . . Who? Would you repeat that? . . . What's your address? . . . What! Yes, indeed, I know where that is. Stay there, I'm sending someone over right away."

"Who was that?" Dickory asked.

Quinn looked puzzled. "I'm not sure. He says he's a friend of yours."

Dickory understood the chief's bewilderment. "That's his real name—George Washington."

Quinn smiled. "I'm glad to hear it; with a name like that, he's got to be telling the truth. He's been trying to reach you to tell you he remembers the name of the tattooed sailor who was blackmailing Mallomar.

Dickory sank back into her chair shaken with pain, stunned by her near escape from death, and sickened by the fumes left by the exterminator and Quinn's cigar. The name of the tattooed sailor was Rossetti!

4

"Hey, Dickory, isn't that where you work?" Her brother Donald sat upright on the couch and pointed to the scene on the late evening news.

Dickory was drawing on a sketch pad. "What?"

"What do you mean, what? Isn't that where you work, at that painter Garson's house, where the murders took place?"

"Murders, what murders?" Blanche asked excitedly.

"I'd rather not talk about it," Dickory replied.

"What do you mean, you'd rather not talk about it?" Donald said parrot-like. He walked to the dining table and took the sketch pad from her hands. "Look at me, Dickory. Were you in any danger there?"

Looking up she saw, not anger, but deep concern. Blanche sat down beside her and wrapped an arm around Dickory's shoulder, drawing her close. "What happened, honey? Please, tell us."

Pulling her turtleneck high on her throat to hide the bruises, Dickory shrugged off their distress. "It's nothing, really. It all happened downstairs of the place where I work, not in the studio." She smiled to put them at ease. "It had nothing to do with me or Garson. The television reporters are making a big fuss over nothing. A gangland killing, that's all it was. Besides, it's over." She had to re-assure them several times more before her brother and sister-in-law were convinced that she was safe in Cobble Lane.

"What are you drawing here?" Donald asked, realizing how little he knew about his kid sister.

"Just a sketch for school," she lied.

"I think it's very good, Dickory," Blanche said, peering over her husband's shoulder.

"Well, it's sure better than that mess with the black dot you did, and the one with the three black lines," Donald said appreciatively. "At least this looks like something. What's it supposed to be, a sailor of some sort?"

"Sure, it's a sailor," Blanche said. "Can't you see the earring in his ear and the tattoo on his arm?"

"Oh yeah," Donald said. "It's one of those old-time sailors like you see in the movies. Pretty good, Dickory." He handed back the sketch pad and yawned. "Think I'll get me to bed. Come on, Blanche."

Refusing their offer to open the couch and help make the bed, Dickory mumbled "Good night" as she studied her sketch. It was not good, not good at all. The figure was awkwardly drawn; the man, lifeless. And Donald was right, the costume was out of a Grade-B Hollywood movie.

Costumes, disguises, that's all she had drawn, not the man, not even the actor beneath the disguise.

The whole scene seemed like a bad movie—the sailor's costume, blackmail, threats, underworld contracts, even the wild coincidence of two people using the name Rossetti. The tattooed sailor must have chosen the name just as she had done, remembering the story Garson had told her. NO! Her thinking was muddled; she would start at the beginning, slowly, methodically, like Sergeant Kod.

Kod was Dock spelled backward, almost, like Noserag/Garson. Huddled at one end of the couch, Dickory doodled around her sketch. She lettered Rossetti and tried it backward; Ittessor meant nothing, no matter how she fudged the letters. Start again.

She had seen Rossetti twice, once on Eighth Street when he had handed her the letter; then, standing over the dead bodies. George had seen Rossetti at a café with Mallomar. Therefore, Rossetti was someone Mallomar knew and someone she knew—or why a disguise?

Rossetti was a blackmailer, or was he a blackmail victim? A blackmail victim who murdered his blackmailer? No. Rossetti was not a murderer. He had threatened Mallomar just to get back the evidence against him. Rossetti was a blackmail victim, a Smith or a Jones, who had saved her life.

Dawn filtered through the dirty windows, waking Dickory from her short sleep. She was still huddled on the couch, sketch pad on her lap. Bleary-eyed and aching, she tossed the drawing of the tattooed sailor to the floor and stretched out to return to forgetfulness. Suddenly she sat up with a start and picked up her pad. A doodled word had screamed out at her: Garson. Gar Son. Ed-GAR SON-neborg.

Edgar Sonneborg, hidden by the large easel, was painting when Dickory arrived. From the studio doorway she watched the back of the canvas heave with the furious strokes of the master artist. Then the canvas was still. Sonneborg threw his crimson-dipped brush upon the pile of squeezed tubes on the messy taboret top, sighed deeply, and covered his canvas with the red velvet drape.

"Hi, Garson," Dickory said.

Startled, Garson stepped away from the easel and stared at her with cold, questioning eyes.

"I just got here," Dickory said quickly, pretending she had noticed nothing. "I—I didn't much feel like going to school."

Garson covered his alarm with a stream of talk. "I did ask for a quiet assistant, didn't I? Poor kid, you probably didn't get a wink of sleep. Neither did I, what with those dreadful happenings right in my own house. I still can't believe it all happened. Honestly, Dickory, if I had any idea you would get involved in this filthy business, I— well, never mind. We're going to find that Rossetti, you'll see. I'm going to paint the most accurate portrait ever painted from eyewitness testimony."

"Garson, I've been thinking," Dickory said. "Rossetti saved my life. Maybe you shouldn't paint his portrait."

Garson did not seem to hear. "Shouldn't paint his portrait? Of course, you are absolutely right. It is Inspector Noserag who will paint the portrait of Rossetti. Quick, Sergeant, the hats."

Still wondering how to get through to him, Dickory put on her helmet and opened a drawer of the inspector's taboret. "Garson, please, it's too late for games. I've—I've seen through your disguise."

Standing rigid as a statue, except for his trembling hand, Garson tried to read her haunted face. "Observant

Dickory, I trained you too well, I'm afraid. The last thing in the world I wanted was for you to get hurt. If only I hadn't told you the story of Christina Rossetti, all this might never have happened. If I hadn't let those thugs live in this house; if I had been home; if, if, if. It's all so complicated, I scarcely know how to tell you about it."

Dickory helped him along. "Why are your paintings kept secret—the Sonneborgs?"

Garson gasped, then emitted a loud, hollow laugh that could have been a cry. Slowly his mask melted away, revealing a sensitive and anguished face, the face Dickory had occasionally glimpsed, the face and now the voice of the Kind One.

"I never imagined you guessed that," he said sadly. "Was it seeing me at the easel this morning?"

"No, I knew before that, Garson." She emphasized the name Garson to prove his secret was safe with her.

"And do you know where the paintings are now?"

"In the locked storeroom, I guess."

Garson nodded. "My lawyer has instructions to protect them, to destroy them if necessary. They must not be shown until all of the sitters are dead."

"But why, Garson?" Dickory argued. "They are great paintings; they must be, if they are anything like the one in the Panzpresser Collection."

"They're better, I'm afraid. Better and crueler. Garson paints people's dreams; Sonneborg shatters them. Shatters them so cruelly that the shards would tear their very souls. No one, Dickory, no one can be confronted with such terrible truth. No one deserves to stand naked and maskless before complete strangers, before the ogling world."

"They are great paintings," Dickory repeated.

"The world can get along without them," Sonneborg

mumbled. "I should have destroyed them long ago. Vanity and greed."

Dickory studied the great artist, the compassionate artist, the guilty artist, with tenderness and awe. He was no real stranger to her. The blue eyes were still blue, but warmer; the waist was still trim. His right hand still shook. His blue jeans were still paint-smeared and the sleeves of his shirt were rolled up. She had not seen his sleeves rolled lately. She had not seen his bare arms lately. Dickory looked down at the open drawer of acrylic paints, paints which could be peeled off the skin, leaving no trace. Five tubes had been used: black (The Case of the Horrible Hairdresser), chrome yellow, chrome green, cadmium red, cobalt blue (the colors of Rossetti's tattoo). The upside-down tattoo, because the artist had painted it on his own arm—on his left arm, so no one would notice his shaky right hand.

"Quick, Inspector Noserag," Dickory shouted to Garson, who was standing before the easel, lost in thought. "We'd better hurry with the portrait of Rossetti so the police can get on his trail."

5

For the first time in the partnership of Noserag and Kod, a portrait of the perpetrator was being painted. The moustache on the manikin was not large enough or dark enough, the striped jersey was the wrong color, the earring was silver, not gold.

"You said Rossetti was thick around the middle, Sergeant?" the artist asked. Dickory had not padded the manikin.

"Very thick. Flabby."

"And his hair and moustache were black?"

"Naturally black, with highlights. Not a wig," she replied with authority.

"Congratulations, Holmes," Chief Quinn boomed, arriving unexpectedly. "I see you have apprehended the suspect." He pointed to the costumed manikin. "Hope you don't mind the intrusion, the kindly police officer at the door let me in."

Noserag and Kod removed their hats. "Either the pipe or the cigar has to go," Dickory said, trying to make light of their embarrassment. "This place has been fumigated enough."

"Speaking of fumigators, Quinn," Garson said, "I thought exterminators needed search warrants these days."

The chief shrugged good-naturedly. "You know how it is, Garson; besides, Detective Finkel didn't take anything. How do you expect us to nail a blackmailer if none of his victims will testify?"

"You don't," Garson retorted. "And while we're at it, how about vandalism—like introducing cockroaches?"

"Somebody did that to you?" the chief exclaimed in mock horror. "Tsk, tsk. If I were you, I'd file a complaint with the authorities. Well, you look better today, Hickory. Let me see, what number are we up to? Six, isn't it?

> "Hickory Dickory Dock,
> The mouse ran up the clock,
> The clock struck six,
> In came the dicks,
> To get Hickory Dickory Dock.

"Dicks, that's what they used to call detectives in the movies," the chief explained.

"I know that," Dickory replied, "but I hope you don't think I murdered Mallomar and Shrimps."

"Everyone is a suspect in a murder case, but don't worry. I have good evidence that you didn't do it."

"Thanks, I'm glad to hear that." Dickory quickly

regretted her sarcasm. They needed the chief on their side. "We've already started on the portrait of the tattooed sailor, Chief Quinn. By the way, what do you call this case?"

"The Case of the Disguised Disguise."

"What?"

"I said, 'The Case of the Disguised Disguise.' "

Chief Quinn had to admit that The Case of the Disguised Disguise was the most baffling case he had ever worked on. "Three things baffled me. First was the description of the tattooed sailor. Four witnesses agreed exactly."

"Four?"

"Hickory, George Washington, the waitress at the café who saw him with Mallomar, and Detective Dinkel."

"Finkel?"

"No, Finkel is the exterminator. I said Dinkel. Detective Dinkel, the derelict who slept across the street, the one following Garson." Garson looked offended. Quinn apologized with a shrug. "How were we to know you weren't the ringleader in the blackmail operation? After all, it was run out of this house. Here, take a look at this, Hickory; we had a police artist make a sketch of Rossetti."

Dickory was critical of the shaded pencil sketch. "It's a clumsy drawing, no life to it, no depth."

"I'm not entering it in an art show," Quinn replied. "Just tell me if this is what Rossetti looks like."

The crude portrait looked like any one of a million men in disguise. "That's him, all right," she said. "That's Rossetti. But it doesn't show his fat waist, or his tattoo."

"Don't worry about the tattoo; we've sent a description to all the tattoo parlors in these parts. That's the second thing that baffles me: the tattoo. Why would any-one want the word Potato tattooed on his arm?"

"Maybe he's a potato freak, like our pistachio-nut ad-dict in The Case of the Face on the Five-Dollar Bill,"
Dickory suggested. "Or maybe his name is Potato. That's no stranger than George Washington."

Quinn was skeptical. "Why didn't Rossetti cover up such an identifiable mark?"

Garson answered that one. "He probably forgot it was there. I once painted a woman who had a four-inch scar on her chin. I asked her if she wanted the scar included in her portrait. 'What scar?' she asked. She had had it since childhood and no longer saw it in the mirror."

The chief shifted his cigar. "Why was the tattoo up-side down?"

Caught by surprise in the middle of a sip of coffee, Garson coughed and spluttered.

"You know, Chief," Dickory said quickly, "when I first saw that tattoo I wondered why all tattoos weren't that way. I wondered why anyone would go to all the bother of having a tattoo needled into his skin if he couldn't read it. I think Rossetti was pretty smart to have an upside-down tattoo that he could read. Maybe his girl friend was the one with the name Potato. Or maybe it was short for Sweet Potato. Come to think of it, the tattoo may have said Patootie."

An inch of ash dropped to the chief's vest. "Thanks a lot, you've both been a big help. Now all I have to do is find a sailor named Potato, who doesn't remember he has a tattoo he can read, who has a sweet patootie."

The third thing that baffled Quinn was Rossetti's dis-appearance after the crime. "No one saw the sailor enter or leave the house, according to Detective Winkle's report."

"Dinkel?" said Garson.

"Not Dinkel, Winkle. Dinkel's the derelict; Winkle is the blind man." Quinn read from Detective Winkle's report:

"Garson left house at 2:30.
   Hickory arrived at 3:00.
   Finkel (exterminator) arrived 3:05, left 3:34.
   Mallomar & Marinara arrived 3:34.
   Hickory ran out at 4:02.
   Police arrived at 4:03.
   Garson arrived 4:45."

"But I saw the sailor; I saw Rossetti," Dickory insisted. "Detective Finkel is wrong."

"Winkle, not Finkel. Finkel is the exterminator," Quinn replied impatiently. "Detective Winkle was probably at the other end of the block when Rossetti entered the house, either waiting for his dog to relieve himself, or soliciting money. He was more interested in how much he collected in his tin cup than in watching Mallomar."

"He owes me a quarter," Dickory said.

The chief sighed. "That Winkle is as bad as Dinkel. Dinkel's been so busy playing derelict he actually fell asleep on the job a couple of times. You don't know the problems I've had getting good street detectives these days."

"Maybe Dinkel didn't see Rossetti leave for the same reason," Dickory suggested.

"Finkel," Garson said, trying to confuse the issue.

"Winkle," snarled Quinn, biting down on his cigar. "You, Hickory, were on the front stoop with Detective Winkle until the police arrived. Right?"

Dickory nodded. "There's a door under the front stoop."

Quinn would not accept that way of escape. "The door to the furnace room was bolted from the kitchen side. No one could have gone through that door and bolted it behind him. Besides, Winkle isn't that blind. He would have seen someone leave from the door under the stoop."

"You mean the murderer is still in this house?" Garson asked, pretending fright.

The chief smiled inscrutably. "Just wanted to hear your views on the problem. You see, I know how the sailor got out of the house."

"How?" Dickory asked. She remembered that Garson had arrived through the police barricade, so he could not have been hiding in the house, not with the police swarming through it.

"How?" Garson asked. "I must admit I can't imagine."

"It was a knotty problem, all right," the chief replied, staring at Garson, "and partly my fault. Too many men with too many confused reports. I had to interview Finkel, Dinkel, and Winkle several times before I had an accurate picture of who was where when."

"Who was where when?" Dickory repeated, confused.

"Who, which officer, Finkel, Dinkel, or Winkle, was where, in what place, at any given moment," Quinn explained. "And do you know what it took to solve it? Humility. I, Joseph P. Quinn, had to question my own testimony and accept the conclusion that I was mistaken. You see, I saw Rossetti leave this house. And so did you, Hickory. And so did Detective Winkle. In fact, half the police force saw Rossetti leave."

"I was in sort of a daze," Dickory said.

"So was I," the chief had to admit. "Remember when Detective Dinkel, the derelict, almost tripped over you coming down the front stoop? Well, I didn't pay much attention, even when he said he was going to check the back of the house. You can't reach the back of the house from the outside. And the real Dinkel was three blocks away at the time, waiting for Garson to leave his health club."

"You mean Rossetti disguised himself as Finkel?" Dickory asked, pleased with Garson's genius.

"Dinkel, not Finkel. Dinkel's the derelict, Finkel's the exterminator," the chief explained once more. "The way I figure it, when Hickory ran out the front door, Rossetti ran upstairs to the costume room, put on a beard like the one Dinkel wears, pulled a torn lumberjack shirt and baggy pants over his sailor's suit, and ran down the stairs and out the front door. In the confusion, everyone, including me, thought it was Detective Dinkel. That's why I call this The Case of the Disguised Disguise."

"Very clever," Garson said, "but I didn't know there was a ragged costume like that upstairs."

"Rossetti deliberately ripped the shirt; and the pants were just too large. It wasn't a perfect imitation, but good enough to pass unnoticed through a mob of police searching for a sailor. Detective Dinkel didn't think that the derelict who went into the health club looked like him at all."

"Probably a different derelict, a real one," Garson said. "There are plenty of derelicts around here these days. Too many. I've been meaning to speak to you about that, Chief."

"Busy place, that health club you go to, Garson. The sailor came out of there, too." Quinn checked another report.

"Sailor left at 3:50.
Derelict entered at 4:10.
Garson left at 4:40."

143

"What are you going to do with Rossetti if you ever find him?" Dickory asked, worried that Quinn was coming too close to the truth. "I mean, he's not really a murderer, you know. He had to kill Mallomar and Shrimps to save my life. Isn't that self-defense or justifiable manslaughter or something like that, Chief? Isn't it?"

Quinn ignored her question. "Another strange thing about this case is the murder weapon, or rather the lack of one. We figured the sailor took it with him. We searched that health club up and down, nearly took the joint apart piece by piece, looking for a blunt instrument. Found all sorts of things, like the derelict's clothes, the sailor's clothes, even the false beard." He walked to the manikin and removed the moustache. "Everything but Rossetti's moustache."

"Rossetti's moustache was bigger and darker than that," Dickory insisted.

"Oh, and paint. We found fragments of acrylic paint in the shower drain." Quinn fingered the tubes on the Noserag taboret top.

"And the murder weapon?" Dickory asked, horrified.

Quinn looked down from the window and brushed cigar ashes from his chest. "There was no murder weapon. Mallomar and Marinara had their heads bashed together. Their skulls were crushed against each other by a pair of large and very strong hands."

Garson did not have large and very strong hands, Dickory thought. And the last time he had threatened Mallomar he had ended up with a black eye. Now there wasn't a scratch on him. She knew only one person strong enough to kill two men barehanded.

Detectives Dinkel, Winkle, and Finkel entered the studio.

Dickory ran to the radiator and banged it with the hammer, again and again.

"Stop, Dickory," Garson shouted. He was restrained by Winkle.

She banged again. If the door to the basement was still bolted, Isaac would break it down to answer his call. She banged again and listened. Heavy footsteps thudded up the stairs.

"I confess, Chief," Garson said, extending his wrists in surrender. "I killed Mallomar and Shrimps."

"Garson didn't do it," Dickory shouted. "He did!" She pointed to the doorway at the huge man staring vacantly into space. "Garson is just protecting Isaac Bickerstaffe."

"Don't bother with him," the chief snapped at Detective Dinkel, who was about to handcuff Garson. "Handcuff the big man; he's the dangerous one." Isaac did look dangerous. He was grunting his horrible grunts, thinking Garson was being set upon.

"Isaac wouldn't hurt a flea," Garson protested. "Besides, he couldn't have committed the murder; the door to the basement was bolted."

"Bolted after the fact," Quinn said. "By a man who called himself Rossetti."

"You know I'm Rossetti," Garson argued. "You can't lock that frightened creature in a jail cell, or put him away to rot in some stinking hole for the mentally retarded. It's me you should arrest. I've already confessed to the murders."

"Sorry, Garson." Quinn motioned to his detectives to take Isaac away. Dinkel and Winkle looked up at the huge, one-eyed monster and wished they had joined up with the fire department instead of the NYPD. To their immense relief, Isaac went quietly.

"Let Isaac stay here in my recognizance," Garson begged. "I'm the only one he can relate to; I'm the only one who can care for him."

"Can't do that, Garson," Quinn replied solemnly. "You see, you are under arrest, too."

"What?" Dickory shouted as Detective Finkel took Garson by the arm.

"Garson, alias Rossetti, alias Frederick Schmaltz," the chief continued, "I place you under arrest for conspiring with known criminals, possible extortion, accessory to murder, and anything else I can think of until. . . ."

"Who's Frederick Schmaltz?" Dickory cried in bewilderment.

"One minute, please," Garson said, unperturbed by the arrest. "Before I am incarcerated for my dastardly deeds, there is an important piece of information I must convey to you." He had never sounded more calm.

"You have a right to remain silent. . . ."

"I am well aware of my rights," Garson replied. "Chief Quinn, I am happy to announce that I have solved another case for you. Eldon F. Zyzyskczuk is not three men, nor is he two men. Eldon F. Zyzyskczuk is a shrewd forger of his own forgeries. He has sandy hair, wears glasses or tinted contact lenses, and writes with the wrong fingers so that his signatures will not be perfect copies. There is one, and only one, Eldon F. Zyzyskczuk."

"Quite right," Quinn replied. "Now, if you would be so kind as to accompany me to my car, I will take you to see him. But I'm afraid you will remain behind bars much longer than Zyzyskczuk will, once we dig up your basement."

"No," Dickory shouted.

Garson placed his shaking hand on Dickory's shoulder. "Chief Quinn, there is no need to dig up the basement. I, Frederick Schmaltz, confess to the murder of Edgar Sonneborg."

The Case of the
Confusing Corpus

1

Number 12 Cobble Lane was once again silent. Manny Mallomar and Shrimps Marinara were dead. Garson and Isaac Bickerstaffe were in jail awaiting trials for murder. Only Dickory remained. Clutching and twisting the red velvet now draped across her lap, she sat before the Sonneborg easel and studied the unfinished canvas.

The painting was unsigned, but it was obviously the work of the same artist who had painted the "Fruit Peddler" in the Panzpresser Collection. The vibrant style was freer, the brushstrokes more confident, but it *was* an Edgar Sonneborg. Edgar Sonneborg had matured into a master.

It was a self-portrait. A double self-portrait. Within

the painting a harsh and distorted Sonneborg was painting a harsh and distorted portrait of Garson. Both faces
had the same features; both stared out at Dickory—Sonneborg's face, twisted by cruelty; Garson's face, arch and
vain. In the blurred right hand of Sonneborg was a paintbrush dipped in alizarin crimson. In the canvas within
the canvas Garson's blurred right hand was covered with
blood. That was what Garson/Sonneborg had been adding to the portrait when she had surprised him at the
easel; he had been painting in the blood.

Dickory understood the blood signified guilt, not
murder. But would anyone else believe that?

The light in the studio was fading rapidly. The blue
of Garson's turtleneck jersey deepened to purple; the
vibrant colors faded to grays. Like a sleepwalker rising
with a dream, Dickory rose and wandered aimlessly about
the darkening studio, back and forth, back and forth, just
like her brother Donald. (Must be a family trait.) She
had wheedled and pleaded with her brother and Blanche,
then just told them that she was going to stay in Cobble
Lane. She had invited them to live with her, but Donald
was too proud to accept charity. The house was hers now,
to live in, to keep forever if Garson never returned; that's
what he had said before being driven off in Quinn's car.
The house, the furniture, the easels and taborets, the
paints and costumes, all belonged to her now. Perhaps
she would invite some of her friends to work in the studio
with her; or she could rent out the downstairs apartment
to George for a minimal fee, like cleaning her brushes and
capping her paints. What happened to George? She hadn't
seen him or heard from him since Mallomar's murder.

Dickory groaned aloud. How could she think such
selfish thoughts when Garson was locked behind bars for
a crime he did not commit?

The telephone rang three times, stopped, and rang again. It was the code only her brother and Chief Quinn knew, devised to protect her from crank calls and inquisitive reporters.

"Hello, Hickory, you all right?"

"Sure, Chief. How's Garson?"

"Fine, just fine; says you shouldn't worry. His lawyer arranged for Isaac Bickerstaffe to be Garson's cellmate. The big fellow seems more at peace now that his friend is with him."

Once again Dickory had forgotten about Isaac. Garson was right; she was uncharitable. "When can I see Garson? And Isaac," she added as an afterthought. "Can they get out on bail?"

"Bail's a bit tricky on a murder charge, and usually only relatives can visit prisoners, but I'll arrange for you to see them in a few days. Meanwhile, I've got some things to discuss with you. Eight in the morning be all right?"

"Eight is fine, Chief. I'm not quite ready to go back to school yet."

"Well, get a good night's sleep. And don't worry; I've got a man watching the house."

"I've seen him, a bearded kid with a backpack and a guitar. He's keeping the whole neighborhood awake with his awful strumming. What's his name, Tinkle?"

"No, Hinkle." Quinn hung up, wondering if he would ever find any competent street detectives.

At eight o'clock sharp, the shiny black car rolled into the narrow street. From the window Dickory watched Chief Quinn climb the stoop. She heard him ring the bell. He had come to question her, possibly to search for evidence that would convict Garson of the murder of Edgar Sonneborg. But there had been no murder. Garson had not killed Sonneborg; Garson *was* Sonneborg. Somehow or other, without revealing his identity or the existence of the paintings, Dickory had to convince the chief that Garson was innocent of the impossible crime.

Quinn rang again. Dickory covered the Sonneborg self-portrait with the red velvet drape and slowly descended the stairs. She wanted Quinn to wait. She was going to take the offensive in her duel with the Chief of Detectives of the New York City Police Department.

"Good morning, Chief Quinn. I was just having coffee in my studio. Won't you join me?" The lady of the manor led her guest up the stairs.

"I just wanted to ask a few questions," Quinn said.

"Please sit down and make yourself comfortable. You take your coffee black, if I remember correctly. Now, where were we? Oh yes, seven."

"Seven?"

"Yes, I am quite certain it was seven. You rhymed six with dicks, but you may not rhyme seven with heaven. I am not about to leave this sunny world just yet." She tossed her head and uttered a brittle laugh.

Phony, just like Garson, Quinn thought, wondering if it was contagious or just came with the house. "Seven, now let me think." He reached into his pocket and pulled out a small object that he kept hidden in his large fist.

> "Hickory Dickory Dock,
>   The mouse ran up the clock,
>   The clock struck seven,
>   Eight, nine, ten, eleven,
>   For Hickory Dickory Dock."

Quinn clicked open the enamel case painted with roses and, dangling the watch from its chain, handed it to Dickory.

"Oranges and lemons,"
    say the bells of St. Clements;
"You owe me five farthings,"
    say the bells of St. Martins,
"When will you pay me?"
    say the bells of Old Bailey,
"When I grow rich,"
    say the bells of Shoreditch.

Eyes closed squeezing back her tears, Dickory shut the case on the antique watch and listened to Quinn's explanation of how Shrimps had been involved in the robbery of Dock's Hock Shop. He had not only stolen the watch after the murder of her parents, but the recording equipment as well.

"Now, Hickory, I'm afraid I have something else for you."

She opened her eyes to a search warrant.

"It's the basement that I'm really interested in," the chief explained. "Do you happen to have the combination to the lock on the storeroom door?"

"Dickory, my name is Dickory," she replied, stalling for time. She had been caught off guard by the old watch and its painful memories; now the chief had the upper hand. She did not have the combination to the lock, but she didn't want him to know that, yet. "Chief, I do want to help. I'll do everything I can to cooperate with the police, because I know Garson is innocent; but I'm very confused. Would you please tell me what's going on?"

"Fair enough, Dickory," Quinn replied sympathetically. He settled back in his chair, unwrapped a cigar, lighted it carefully, then began his tale.

"Julius Panzpresser first called my attention to the disappearance of Edgar Sonneborg at a dinner party a month or so ago. Sonneborg had been missing for fifteen years, but I put a man on the case anyway—Panzpresser is a very influential person, you know. Well, much to my surprise, things got moving pretty fast. The more we found out, the more suspicious we became."

"What did you find out?" Dickory asked.

"First we tracked down the private detective that had worked on this case for Panzpresser—Manny Mallomar."

"Mallomar, a private detective?"

Quinn nodded. "He was, until he found out he could make more money in the extortion racket. Mallomar refused to tell us anything about Sonneborg, but we were curious about his living in Garson's house. Why would a well-known artist rent half of his house to two crooks like Manny Mallomar and Shrimps Marinara? So, we checked Garson's bank records. Garson's a wealthy man; he didn't need rent money; in fact, there were no deposits to account for rent. But he was withdrawing large sums regularly. Blackmail. Then when we saw Panzpresser enter this house, we were certain it was blackmail."

"Cookie came here to sit for her portrait," Dickory said.

"Not Cookie, her husband, Julius. Mallomar was not only blackmailing Garson, but Julius Panzpresser and quite a few other people as well."

Dickory wondered which of the Smiths or Joneses was Julius Panzpresser.

The chief continued. "As far as we could tell, Garson was the only artist Mallomar was blackmailing. And Mallomar had worked on the Sonneborg case. We figured Garson, the artist, knew something about Sonneborg, the artist, and was paying dearly to keep it secret. I decided to dig into Garson's past, and keep an eye on his present comings and goings."

Now Dickory realized why the chief had visited their

studio so often. It was not because he wanted their help on his cases. "You were spying on Garson!"

Quinn tapped cigar ash into his coffee cup. He did not like the word "spying." "Surveillance," he said. "We had come across some incriminating evidence and I was trying to figure out how Garson's mind worked. A fascinating mind, very shrewd, very clever. In fact, I rather enjoyed his Sherlock Holmes deductions."

"What incriminating evidence?"

"When last seen, Edgar Sonneborg shared an attic studio with another young artist, Frederick Schmaltz. That was fifteen years ago, and neither has been heard from since. Their landlady is long dead, but her son remembers seeing one of the artists lugging a heavy trunk down the stairs. He remembers the exact date because he had come to the house for his mother's birthday. It was September tenth. September tenth," the chief repeated, "and the landlady's son identified a photograph of Garson as the artist he saw."

"He identified Garson as Frederick Schmaltz?" Dickory asked. She knew that was impossible, Garson was Sonneborg. But what had become of Frederick Schmaltz?

The chief hedged the question. "The landlady's son identified the photograph as one of the two artists who lived in the attic, and the last one seen. The artist who moved out a large heavy trunk on September tenth was Garson, and on September tenth of the same year, Garson moved into this house."

"That's not evidence for murder," Dickory said derisively.

"No, it may not be evidence," Quinn had to admit, "but it is a fact. And we do have the tape recording."

Mallomar had been blackmailing Garson with a tape. Somehow or other, Shrimps had bugged the office of

Garson's lawyer, and the police had found the tape recording in Mallomar's files. Quinn shuffled through a notebook. "Funny thing, of all the dirt Mallomar collected against his victims, this was the only one of criminal nature. Everybody else was paying for stupid indiscretions. We destroyed all that, of course."

"Read me what was on the tape," Dickory said impatiently.

"Ah, here we are." Quinn cleared his throat and read the fragmentary transcript. "The corpus of Edgar Sonneborg (unintelligible) basement of Number 12 Cobble Lane (unintelligible) kept secret at all costs (unintelligible) death of all concerned."

"Corpus!" Dickory gasped.

"That means body," the chief explained.

Dickory knew corpus meant body; corpus was often used in discussing the complete life's work of an artist. The transcript meant that the body of the work of Edgar Sonneborg (his paintings) must be kept from public display until all of the persons in the portraits were dead. But she could not tell Chief Quinn that, not without revealing the existence of the Sonneborg canvases. "A tape recording cannot be used as evidence," she said, unsure of her facts.

Quinn shrugged. "You forget, Hickory, that Garson has confessed."

2

The lock had been sawed, the door broken in by the time Dickory and Chief Quinn reached the basement storeroom. The police were awaiting orders from the chief.

Except for the racks against the walls holding unframed canvases, the room was bare. Dickory held her breath as Quinn pulled the left edge of one of the Sonneborg paintings halfway from its stack and frowned at what he saw. He much preferred Garson's pretty portraits to this new-fangled modern art.

"Do you like it, Chief?" Dickory said hastily, noticing that the signature was still concealed. "That's one of my paintings, or I guess I should say one of my attempts at painting."

"Very nice, Hickory, for a beginner. Nice, bright color. I like it." Embarrassed by his lie, Quinn quickly slid the painting back into the rack and ordered his men to dig up the concrete floor. After all, he was looking for a corpus, not a masterpiece.

The Sonneborg paintings were safe, for the while.

The police dug a six-foot hole in the storeroom floor, dug up the cement around the furnace, dug up the tile in the kitchen and the floorboards in the spare room. All they found were some old whiskey bottles hidden in the prohibition years and a skeleton of a dead mouse.

"There's your corpus, Chief," Dickory said.

Quinn bit hard on his cigar stub and stormed out of the house, leaving a crew to repair the damaged floors.

Hat on her head, Sergeant Kod sat on a packing case in the middle of the storeroom surrounded by the Sonneborg paintings she had removed from the racks. Souls, naked in unrelenting truth, stared out at her from their canvases as she tried to untangle the knots of this non-existent case. There were no witnesses, no descriptions, just these paintings in the basement and the Sonneborg self-portrait upstairs in the studio, the double self-portrait with the bloodstained hand.

Sonneborg was Garson, but how could she prove that without revealing these paintings? Sonneborg was Garson, but who was Frederick Schmaltz?

A drum majorette laughed uproariously as she flung her baton in the air; a jockey rode twelve bent men, whipping his jury with malicious frenzy. Dickory turned away from the portraits of Cookie Panzpresser and Garson's lawyer to seek out the paintings in Sonneborg's earlier style. A strutting matador. A toothy Lady Dracula. A tragic clown dancing with a broken paintbrush and an empty palette. The packing case overturned with a loud thud as Dickory leaped to her feet. That was it! That was the painting she had been looking for—the portrait of Frederick Schmaltz.

Even though Dickory now had proof that Garson was Sonneborg, there was only one person who could help her and still keep the secret. But it was the one person who most wanted Garson behind bars. She rested the two wrapped canvases at her feet and rang the bell of the large mansion.

"I must see Julius Panzpresser immediately," she said to the butler who opened the door.

"I'm sorry, you will have to make an appointment."

She stuck one foot between the jamb and the closing door. "I'm certain Mr. Panzpresser will want to see me. My name is Dock, former secretary to Manny Mallomar. Tell him I have come to discuss a Mr. Smith."

Dickory bit a fingernail to the quick, waiting, hoping she had used the right name. She had. Mr. Smith appeared, his turkey-neck red with anger, and showed her into his study.

She detested this dirty role of blackmailer, but Garson's freedom was at stake. Seated across from her, Panzpresser glared with curiosity and contempt. "The police said they destroyed Mallomar's files," he said at last.

"Photostats," Dickory replied tersely.

"It was a stupid mistake I made years ago. Nothing serious, as you know, but it would be very painful for my wife if she ever found out." Panzpresser looked for sympathy from his young blackmailer, but her face was hard and determined. "All right, how much do you want?"

"We'll get to the price after you've answered a few questions," she said in a businesslike tone. Panzpresser was at her mercy. "First, did you ever meet Edgar Sonneborg?"

"No."

Disappointed, Dickory continued. "Then how did you get his painting, the 'Fruit Peddler'?"

"It won first prize for unexhibited artists at the old Whitney Museum. I bought it."

"But you never met the artist who painted it?"

"Sonneborg? No, I never met Sonneborg. The painting was delivered by a friend of his, another artist who wanted to show me some of his own paintings. They were awful. The only good thing about them was the frames. I suggested he give up painting and become a framemaker."

"What was this friend's name?" Dickory asked from the edge of her chair.

"Name? How should I know, that was fifteen years ago."

Dickory unwrapped the paintings and held one toward Julius Panzpresser. "Is this the friend?"

"Sonneborg!" Panzpresser exclaimed to Dickory's horror. He leaped up, grabbed the painting, and rushed to the window to examine it in daylight. "Where did you get this? This is a Sonneborg painting!"

"Yes, Mr. Panzpresser, this is a Sonneborg painting," Dickory said with relief. "But who is the man in the portrait?"

The art collector was so delighted with his new discovery that Dickory had to repeat her question.

"The man in the portrait? Oh, that's the big guy who delivered the 'Fruit Peddler,' the one with the good frames."

"His name was Frederick Schmaltz," Dickory said. "His name is now Isaac Bickerstaffe, though his face is hardly recognizable. He saved my life."

"Fifteen years I've been searching for another Sonneborg painting. Fifteen years." Eyes glued to the canvas, he had not heard a word Dickory said.

"Mr. Panzpresser, please put that painting down. I have some very important things to discuss with you. Mr. Panzpresser. Photostats! Blackmail!"

The art collector returned to his chair, more concerned about buying the painting than paying blackmail. "Name your price."

"Free Garson."

"Garson!" Panzpresser was out of his chair again, ranting about that third-rate dabbler, that murderer who deprived the world of one of its great modern geniuses. Only after Dickory started for the door with both canvases did he settle down and listen to her explanation.

"I don't have any photostats, Mr. Panzpresser, and even if I did I would never blackmail anybody. But I had to get you to hear my story. You have a great deal of influence; you could get Garson released from prison—after all, you started the whole investigation."

Julius Panzpresser began fuming again.

"Edgar Sonneborg is still alive. And still painting," she said quickly.

Now Julius listened.

Dickory explained, upon Panzpresser's promise of secrecy, that Garson was Sonneborg. She explained why Garson insisted that the paintings be kept from public view.

The art collector was still skeptical. "Even if I could identify the mutilated man, Isaac what's-his-name, as the one who delivered the painting, it doesn't prove he's Schmaltz. Besides, this painting is of the same period as the 'Fruit Peddler.' That ridiculous portrait Garson made of my wife looks more like the work of Schmaltz than the genius of Sonneborg."

Dickory was prepared for this argument. "Mr. Panzpresser, I have met your wife, Cookie. She is a wonderful woman, so cheerful and full of life."

"Oh, no," Julius moaned. "Not blackmail again."

"Not at all. I don't want to hurt either you or Mrs. Panzpresser; I just want to free Garson." Dickory unwrapped the second canvas. "I have something to show you that may cause you some pain, but please try to look at it with the eye of a collector. Look at it for the masterpiece it is, one of the greatest paintings of Edgar Sonneborg."

Julius Panzpresser stared into the laughing face of a prancing, middle-aged drum majorette, hat askew on her tousled bleached curls.

"Cookie," he said. "That's my Cookie."

3

Wearing the blank mask of Garson, Edgar Sonneborg sat opposite Dickory behind the glass partition. He looked grayer, slimmer, in his baggy prison chinos. His right hand shook noticeably as he lifted the telephone to speak.

"Isaac and I will be released in a day or two. Chief Quinn said you arranged the whole thing."

Dickory squirmed in her chair. "It was really Julius Panzpresser who did it." Eyes lowered, she explained in a hesitant voice, "I—I exchanged the Garson portrait of Cookie serving tea for the Sonneborg painting of the drum majorette."

Garson turned ashen.

"Don't worry, Garson. Please," she whispered into

the phone. "I had to do it to get you out of here. You and Isaac. Julius Panzpresser promised never to show the portrait to anyone. Or to tell anyone that Sonneborg is still alive."

Slumped in his chair, Garson did not respond.

"No one was hurt, Garson, just the opposite. You see, you were wrong about Cookie. In the Garson portrait you painted her, not as she saw herself, but as she thought her husband wanted her to be. Neither you nor Cookie realized that Julius Panzpresser loves his wife just as she is—happy and nutty, just as she is in the Sonneborg portrait." Dickory tried a smile. "Now they're both happy and nutty and off on their second honeymoon."

"Well, I guess I can't complain about a happy ending," Garson said listlessly. He looked tired and drawn.

"Is it awful in here?" Dickory asked with concern.

He tried to put her at ease with a shrug. "Not really, but I do miss not being able to work. There are so many characters here I'd like to paint. Recognize anybody?"

For the first time since entering the visitors' room Dickory noticed the other prisoners seated in a row behind the glass partition, speaking in telephones to their relatives. At the far end she did recognize somebody— Professor D'Arches. He was shouting with great agitation to an attractive woman, probably his wife, who seemed to be taking it all in stride. Next to D'Arches sat a chubby young man, Harold Silverfish, who was trying to console an even chubbier visitor, his sad-faced mother.

"They were arrested for tearing down the traffic signs on Wall Street," Garson explained. "They'll be released as soon as bail is posted. Now, do you recognize the next man?"

The prisoner looked familiar to Dickory—elderly, portly, she had seen him somewhere before—standing in a photograph. "F. K. Opalmeyer?"

Garson nodded.

"Good old Opalmeyer and the Empress Fatima brace-let," Dickory said. The next prisoner she recognized from the bobbed nose that didn't fit his face. And his red thumbs. "Winston S. Fiddle, the face on the five-dollar bill."

"Very good. Now, do you recognize the one and only?" Garson pointed to a middle-aged prisoner who had just sat down. Sandy hair, rimless glasses, Dickory could not remember having seen his face before. But she did recognize his gangly visitor who was entering the room. "George!"

"Hi, Dickory," George Washington III said sheepishly. He walked toward her with a reddened face. "I'm visiting my uncle."

"Your uncle?"

He nodded, still blushing. "He got himself into a lot of trouble for having two different apartments and not paying his bills. I can't quite figure it out, Dickory. Seems he was forging his own name, if you can do such a thing."

Now Dickory recognized the prisoner. "Eldon F. Zy-zyskczuk," she exclaimed.

"How did you know that?" George asked in amazement. "He's from the side of the family that didn't change their name."

"Your uncle Eldon is a very famous man," Dickory said. "Why don't you wait outside for me when your visit is over, George, and we'll go for some pizza. And then to work. We've got a lot of assignments to catch up on."

A happier George walked over to his uncle, and Dickory returned to Garson. "How is Isaac?" she asked.

Isaac was not well. "He has barely eaten," Garson said sadly, "and he never smiles. He doesn't know where he is, or that he'll soon be going home."

Julius Panzpresser, having twisted a few arms, had

arranged for the deaf-mute's release in Garson's custody; but Dickory still had some unanswered questions. Isaac was the clue to Garson's guilt, to his bloodstained hand; but she could never ask Garson. "Inspector Noserag, tell me about Frederick Schmaltz," she said.

Garson nodded, then with shoulders slumped and back bowed from years of tracking footprints, Noserag spoke: "Fifteen years ago two struggling young artists shared a studio. They painted from the same models; they sang together and drank together, and together wallowed in shallow profundities. Their names were Edgar Sonneborg and Frederick Schmaltz. Sonneborg had all the talent; Schmaltz had all the charm, but as Sonneborg began to attain some recognition for his work, Schmaltz began to brood. Something in Schmaltz couldn't bear the idea that he would never be another Matisse. Then Sonneborg won the Whitney prize, and Schmaltz's entry was rejected." Garson stopped, his eyes staring into the past.

"Go on, Inspector Noserag."

"Sorry, Sergeant Kod. As I was saying, Schmaltz brooded. Grasping one last chance, he delivered Sonneborg's painting to the art collector who had purchased it, in order to show his own paintings to him. I don't know what Panzpresser told him, but Schmaltz returned to the studio roaring drunk. That night he had the terrible accident."

"It was Panzpresser's fault," Dickory said. "Panzpresser told him that his paintings were awful and he should become a framemaker."

Garson shook his head and closed his eyes against the dreaded memory. "Schmaltz had received criticism before, lots of it. It was later, in the studio, that he—when he saw the portrait Sonneborg was painting, the cruel portrait of Schmaltz as an untalented clown. . . ."

"What happened then, Inspector?" Dickory asked before Garson broke down.

Noserag replied quickly. "Schmaltz ran out into the street, in front of a moving truck. He was drunk, but it was no accident. He tried to kill himself, and he did. He killed Frederick Schmaltz. Only a grunting vegetable survived."

"And that's when Sonneborg became Garson," Dickory guessed.

"Soon after. Schmaltz's parents, who were then alive, wanted to put him in an asylum. Sonneborg changed his named to Garson, renamed Schmaltz, and with the prize money and the Panzpresser fee bought the house on Cobble Lane." Garson rose abruptly. "I'll go with the guard to get him. Isaac just huddles in a corner and won't move unless I lead him. Maybe if he sees you. . . ." His voice broke.

Dickory watched the guilt-ridden artist leave through the barred door of the visitors' room. Another prisoner entered and began pacing back and forth, waiting for his visitor to arrive, back and forth, back and forth.

"Donald!" Dickory shouted, leaping up from her chair.

Her brother Donald could not hear Dickory's shout through the glass. Back and forth he paced as Blanche entered the visitors' section, sobbing.

"Blanche, what's wrong?" Dickory cried, embracing her sister-in-law. "Why is Donald here—in prison?"

"Oh, Dickory, it's just awful," Blanche sobbed. "I don't know how it happened. The electric company turned off the lights again, and Donny went to pay the bill, and they arrested him. Because of his red thumbs. I kept telling him not to eat so many pistachio nuts, you've heard me tell him, Dickory. Poor Donny."

Dickory tried to make some sense out of Blanche's stammerings. "Who arrested him?"

"They did. They arrested poor Donny for passing a counterfeit five-dollar bill. The police searched the whole apartment and everything, but Donny won't tell them where he got it."

The phony five-dollar bill had come from Dickory's dresser drawer. "Don't worry, Blanche; I can fix everything. Donald thinks he is protecting me, that's why he won't say anything. Now, go tell Donald it's all right; I can fix everything. After I leave here, I'll call Chief of Detectives Quinn and tell him it was my five-dollar bill. He'll get Donald out of here, fast." Dickory knew that the chief was accountable for his own evidence. She reassured Blanche several more times, led her to a seat, and threw a kiss to her brother. "Now don't worry."

"Thanks, Dickory," Blanche said, giving her a big hug. "We both miss you so terribly. Are you coming back home soon?"

"No, I'll be living in the downstairs apartment in Garson's house, but I'll come visit the two of you often."

Blanche wiped her eyes and blew her nose, but she still seemed unconsolable.

"Here, Blanche, I almost forgot." Dickory reached into her pocket. "I have a present for you."

Blanche gasped. "But it belongs to you, Dickory."

"It belongs to you now, Blanche. To you and Donald. I owe you a lot." Dickory opened the enameled watchcase painted with roses and placed it into her sister-in-law's hand.

> "Oranges and lemons,"
>   say the bells of St. Clements;
> "You owe me five farthings,"
>   say the bells of St. Martins. . . .

The antique pocket watch was still chiming when Garson returned, shadowed by the shambling Isaac. Head bent, he seemed smaller, as though he had shriveled up into himself. Garson seated the deaf-mute in the chair before Dickory.

He did not look up.

Dickory stared at the poor helpless creature who had saved her life, and whom she had handed over to the police. She was overwhelmed with a confusion of pity and gratitude and guilt, but there was no way she could reach him. She could not touch him through the glass barrier; she could not speak to him over the telephone. She rapped on the glass. She stamped her feet on the floor.

Isaac felt the vibrations and raised his head. His good eye shone glassy and unseeing.

Dickory opened her face into the widest smile she could muster and waved her hand in a happy greeting.

Isaac furrowed his brow.

Dickory held up one finger, meaning wait, bent down and brought her purse up to the tabletop. Isaac's eye moved, following her exaggerated motions.

Dickory opened her purse. She took out a notepad and pencil. She tore off a sheet of paper. She indicated to him that she was going to write a note.

Isaac nodded in slow recognition.

Dickory wrote in bold block letters and held her message against the glass for Isaac to read. She pointed to herself, then to the paper. To herself, to the paper. To herself, to the paper.

Isaac leaned his large frame close to the partition, his scarred face touched the glass and backed away.

Once again Dickory pointed to herself, then to the paper. She smiled broadly.

Isaac traced the shape of each letter with his finger; his lips moved silently, his injured brain struggled with the words. Then he looked up and pointed to Dickory.

Dickory nodded and pointed once again to the paper.

A loud howl erupted from the crippled mute like a clap of wondrous thunder. He rocked in his chair and threw back his head, uttering cries that echoed through the room. Dickory could hear his "ung-ung-ung" through the thick glass. Isaac Bickerstaffe was laughing.

Professor D'Arches looked up; Harold Silverfish looked up; F. K. Opalmeyer looked up; Winston S. Fiddle looked up; Eldon F. Zyzyskczuk looked up; Donald Dock looked up. They laughed along with the laughing Isaac. And Blanche and George and Professor D'Arches' wife and even Harold Silverfish's mother laughed. Isaac pointed to the note. One finger traced a circle, then two fingers climbed the air and down again. He pointed to Dickory and laughed some more. Dickory's heart was like a singing bird.

Garson clapped his big friend on the shoulder, smiled lovingly at his apprentice, and picked up the phone to speak to her.

"Good work, Sergeant," Inspector Noserag intoned. "Your dexterous detection and meritorious compassion have earned you a promotion. Congratulations, Captain Kod."

> Hickory Dickory Dock,
> The mouse ran up the clock,
>   The happy quote
>   On the note she wrote
> Said, "I am Dickory Dock."